La Tour Dreams
of the
Wolf Girl

La Tour Dreams
of the
Wolf Girl

David Huddle

HOUGHTON MIFFLIN COMPANY

BOSTON · NEW YORK

2002

For information about permission to reproduce selections
from this book, write to Permissions, Houghton Mifflin Company,
215 Park Avenue South, New York, New York 10003.

Visit our Web site: www.houghtonmifflinbooks.com.

Library of Congress Cataloging-in-Publication Data
Huddle, David, date.
La Tour dreams of the wolf girl / David Huddle.
p. cm.
ISBN 0-618-08173-9
1. La Tour, Georges du Mesnil de, 1593–1652 — Appreciation — Fiction.
2. Women art historians — Fiction. 3. Artists' models — Fiction.
4. Wild women — Fiction. I. Title.
PS3558.U287 L23 2001
813'.54 — dc21   2001016915

Printed in the United States of America

Book design by Robert Overholtzer

QUM 10 9 8 7 6 5 4 3 2 1

Portions of this novel appeared in issues 28
and 30 of *American Short Fiction.*

*Thanks to Bill Clegg, Janet Silver,
Heidi Pitlor, Elaine Segal,
Frances Apt, and
Lindsey, Bess, and Molly Huddle.*

FOR GHITA ORTH

The dusty old municipal records also reveal a difficult man who, particularly in his later years, was not exactly a model of civic virtue. There were complaints that he refused to contribute his quota to the poor while a famine raged, that he assaulted a sergeant at arms, and that he administered a savage beating to a peasant. One particularly detailed set of charges reported La Tour "making himself obnoxious to everyone by the great number of dogs he keeps, acting as though he were the lord of the manor, sending his dogs after hare into the standing crops, which they trample down and ruin."

— "From Darkness into Light: Rediscovering Georges de La Tour"
Helen Dudar, *Smithsonian,* December 1996, p. 80.

La Tour Dreams

of the

Wolf Girl

I

PROFESSOR NELSON can't get free of Stevens Creek, Virginia. Nine miles west of the Blue Ridge Parkway, marked on only the most detailed maps, it's a cluster of maybe a hundred houses, a store, and two filling stations. During her childhood, the hamlet had two or three times as many of its young men serving time in the penitentiary as it had students attending college. Hostility was part of its weather, but she was never that way. Quiet though she was, Suzanne always wanted to be close to somebody. Her two older sisters, Bonnie and Gail, turned cold toward her when they were little, though Suzanne still tries to be companionable to them. On their birthdays, she sends her sisters cards, but they forget hers every year. At Christmas she buys gifts for them and their kids, knowing that she will receive neither gifts nor thank-you notes.

Her parents are friendly, but in a superficial way. They're guarded in their dealings with her; when Suzanne calls them to chat, she senses how they maneuver to end the conversation.

The estrangements hurt Suzanne. Distant as her life is from theirs, she's done nothing to warrant her sisters' unfriendliness, nor has she ever given her parents cause to be wary of her. How could she help being the freak of the family? She didn't realize that she was smarter — a lot smarter — than her sisters and her parents until she was in eighth grade. That's when she had to ride the school bus thirty-five miles a day, to and from the consolidated high school. The teachers there who'd taught Bonnie and Gail were so stunned by Suzanne's ability that they told her, compared with her sisters, she was a genius. Compared with most of the children who rode the bus in from Stevens Creek to Galax, Suzanne was a female Einstein.

Of course she's the only one in her family who doesn't have that mountain accent — her intuition obliterated it, starting with her first day of eighth grade. People in Galax spoke a more sophisticated version of Appalachian English than did people in Stevens Creek. The way the town kids mocked the country kids was so ruthless that most of Suzanne's Stevens Creek school-bus acquaintances became predictably hostile and all the more determined to hold on to their mother tongue. Suzanne was the only one who began adapting.

It was a talent she had — listening, analyzing, imitating. By her sophomore year, the only ones mocking her way of speaking were a few of the more surly Stevens Creek kids, who took her Galaxized speech as a sign of betrayal. Mostly, though, the Stevens Creek kids thought of her as the one who could compete in that school, the one who had a chance of beating the Galax snobs at their own game.

Nowadays Suzanne is pretty certain that the reason she changed her speech was to make friends among the smart kids. It didn't work. She was popular. Again and again she found herself in groups of Galax girls; she was invited to spend the night at this girl's house and that one's. She made an effort to cultivate the friendship of several girls she admired, but intimacy never developed. She came to see how jokes and manners and the slangy small talk of the day were actually ways of pushing people away. Stevens Creek boys didn't ask her out because she was too smart; Galax boys didn't ask her out because she lived eighteen miles away. Her remembrance of that time in her life is like a nightmare, with her frantically running toward a familiar boy or girl who smiled and beckoned but who then was sucked backward through space, so that no matter how tirelessly she ran, she could never close the distance.

There was, however, the Mute. The Limeberrys, his family, had lived on the outskirts of Stevens Creek for as long as anybody could remember. But the Mute had a foreign look — dark skin, converging eyebrows, a beak-like nose, eyes with whites that caught your attention. The Mute could speak, but there was a nasal harshness to his voice — it sounded as if his words were squeezing through some weird tube behind his nose. From his first day in first grade, he'd been brutally teased. By fourth grade, he'd shut up. He shook his head when his teachers called on him. He'd do that, shake his head yes or no, if you politely asked him a yes-or-no question. He did his homework, all of it printed neatly. When he absolutely had to communicate with a teacher, he'd print a quick note and carry it to the teacher's desk. The Mute also learned to fight well enough — that is, he could exact enough pain — to convince the school bullies to lay off him. Thus, he became a completely isolated boy. In his classes and on the playground, in the cafeteria and the hallways, he moved among the children, but no one spoke with him. No one, as his teachers and the school administrators put it, *interacted* with him. He wasn't antisocial, as far as anyone knew; he just didn't carry out spoken intercourse with anyone. The Mute made himself almost invisible.

What took place between Suzanne and the Mute seemed,

at the time, just something that happened. In retrospect she thinks it may have been the most significant moment in her five years at Blue Ridge High School. That first August morning of eighth grade, when she got on the school bus behind Bonnie and Gail — of course they'd pushed ahead of her — there was no place to sit. She couldn't know it then, but for a Stevens Creek kid, the most brutal politics of high school life had to do with where you sat on the school bus. So there she was, standing at the front, one step past the driver, looking down the aisle all the way to the back, and there was no place for her. There were several empty spaces, but each was a window seat being saved by the kid sitting on the aisle. Among all the faces staring at her, there wasn't a friendly one. Bonnie and Gail each had a pal who'd saved a seat; now they sat staring at her, too, with that gleeful look Suzanne recognized as pure sibling vengefulness. She felt her face reddening. She was twelve years old and probably the youngest kid on the whole bus. She had on her new first-day-of-school dress, and she didn't think there was anything wrong with how she looked, but there was no way she could make somebody give her a seat. She glanced over her shoulder. The bus driver was waiting for her, watching in his mirror to be sure she was seated before he started the bus moving. Twenty-some pairs of eyes blazed at her. She was about to open her mouth to let out what she knew would be a yelp, a wail, a shriek, a moan. That was when the Mute scooted over and gave her a place.

When she had settled into the seat, she murmured, "Thank you, Elijah." She didn't say what any other kid would have said: "Thanks, Mute." She was taking a chance, saying his whole name instead of the nickname Lige, which she somehow knew he wanted to be called. From far back in school, when he was still willing to speak, she must have remembered his telling someone that was his name. Since first grade, they'd been in the same classroom. She remembered a whole catalogue of humiliations he had suffered from their schoolmates over the years. She'd never spoken cruelly to him or done him any harm, but she'd never tried to help or defend him, either. She was his witness. That was what she meant to convey by using his full and proper first name — that and her extreme gratitude, which "Lige" would not have signaled. "Lige" was merely "Thanks," whereas "Elijah" was "Oh, my dear schoolmate, I can never adequately thank you for the noble gesture you just made in that most painful moment of my twelve years of life." And her gratitude was only slightly diminished by her suspicion that he had taken the seat-saving aisle position to avoid the shame of having every bus rider turn down the open seat beside him.

She thought about Elijah while she sat beside him for the long ride to Blue Ridge High School. What kind of parents named their child Elijah? Well, she knew what kind. Religious. And she thought about Elijah's last name: Limeberry. She couldn't imagine how anyone ever got to be named Limeberry, and in her concentration on such matters as his family and his name and the history of suffering that had produced his silence, Suzanne received — as if it were a divine revelation — a blast of empathy. She could feel exactly what it was — even down to the thuds of his heartbeat, his breathing, his body odor, his flat butt on the vinyl seat, and his dozens of unspoken remarks — to be Elijah Limeberry. The transmission of that boy's life into her life lasted no more than about fifteen seconds, but it gave Suzanne a brief spasm of shivers.

So for the five years until they graduated they rode the school bus together each morning. In the afternoon, Suzanne got out of sixth period with enough time to make it onto the bus and claim her own seat. If she'd chosen to sit with Elijah, or if he'd chosen to sit with her for the second time in a single day, they'd have been accused of being "in love." She understood the absurdity — and maybe even the kindness of it. The bus kids allowed them the morning ride together because it was necessary — it was what they had to do to survive — and every kid riding with them understood that. But they wouldn't tolerate Suzanne and Elijah openly choosing each other's company.

So now, when she got on the bus, Elijah automatically scooted over to the window seat to make room. He'd always sit over there, curled away from her and everyone else, and that gave him a little pocket of privacy. He did something with his notebook while he sat there. Suzanne didn't make much of that — most kids did their homework on the bus. For a lot of them it was the only time they ever did homework. Suzanne herself always read on the bus, though it was usually a book that didn't have anything to do with her classes. She read, and he did whatever he did. That was how it was, because within a few weeks after that first morning, they had settled into an unsentimental acknowledgment of their arrangement. She even found herself occasionally slipping back into thinking of him not as Lige or Elijah, but as what he was called by everyone else on that bus — the Mute. And Elijah had gone back to meeting her eyes only for the small moment each morning when she got on the bus and he scooted over. There were no further exchanges.

But that morning on the bus, for whatever reason, she happened to glance his way. At the time it seemed a coincidence; she didn't mean to look at his notebook, and he didn't mean to reveal it. What she saw astonished her; he'd drawn a boy struggling with a monster before a crowd of faces. In her momentary view of the picture, Suzanne saw that the struggling boy was Elijah and that her face was at the front of the crowd. He'd even drawn her fingers touching her mouth to suggest concern and horror. The other faces were fixed in demonic grins. The monster, however, was the dominant image: many-eyed and many-handed, a dark mass of slime that evidently could wrap itself around the boy, take hold of his arms, legs, neck, and torso, envelope him in utter shadow. Quite clearly, the monster would prevail in their struggle. And the boy's — Elijah's — face held an expression of noble determination. One fist was poised for a blow toward a pair of the monster's eyes. The other hand pushed away a grasping set of dark fingers. But anyone could see that the fight couldn't last more than an instant or two. Elijah was about to be consumed by the slimy darkness.

He caught her staring at the picture. Their eyes met and held for a few uncomfortable moments, as if he'd caught her secretly trying to hurt him. But of course she hadn't been doing that. Even now, Suzanne can't think of the word for what passed between them in that look, though it was something like a contract. He agreed to let her know that drawing pictures was what he did, and she agreed not to talk about it with anyone. Well, of course there were no words to the understanding, but that had to be it, because she never did tell anyone, and Elijah did allow her, from time to time, to see his pictures. What she really wanted was to watch him draw, but he never did so in front of her. He might add a little touch of shading if she was looking. When he was really concentrating, he turned away and curled over the notebook, as if he created the drawing within a secret cavity of his body. He worked with a blue pen and a black pen, and sometimes, when his shoulders made a certain movement, Suzanne was pretty certain he was switching from one pen to the other.

When Suzanne recalls their unspoken agreement, she realizes that if Elijah revealed a drawing to her, he did so in a way that would prevent any other kid from seeing it. And she was unobtrusive in her looking. Actually, in the hundreds of mornings they rode the bus together, he probably showed her only a dozen pictures. And when he did, the two of them shielded the picture from the sight of the kids around them. What amazes her is that as intricate as the arrangement was, she gave little thought to it once she stepped off the school bus. Perhaps in the mornings, as she stood by the road waiting for the bus, she wondered what bizarre vision Elijah might show her that day. But during her school hours, and while she was at home, there was no place in her thoughts for Elijah "Lige" Limeberry, a.k.a. the Mute. It was as if she stashed him away in a special compartment of her mind.

That remembrance disturbs her now. What is it about those long-ago days that nags at her? At first she can't grasp it, but as she pushes her memory of Elijah, it begins to take hold. His pictures have lingered in her mind. They are there — is that right? Even now, she holds vivid images that she knows were drawn by Elijah's hand. Except that isn't right, either, because several of the black and blue images in her mind were *not* drawn by Elijah. She herself made them up.

Suzanne begins to see certain parts of her daily life in terms of Elijah's pictures. Or she remembers pieces of her experience as if Elijah had drawn them.

One day at lunch, there was a fight between two Galax boys, football players, in which the one ripped the other's shirt, and the other screamed foul names and brandished a cafeteria chair. Suzanne saw the fight, and she knows Elijah didn't — because unless the weather was freezing cold, he always took his brown bag outdoors to eat by himself. But she remembers that fight as if Elijah had drawn it, the fighters looming, huge and furious, one boy's veins popping in his neck as he stood cursing the other. Elijah would have shown the faces in the background

— maybe one of them hers — and he would have shown the vice-principal pushing his way through the crowd to stop the fight and take the boys to the office, even though that didn't really happen.

The only pictures Elijah showed Suzanne were related to school. He drew one that is as clear in her memory as if it were a painting she had studied and written about. It was of Mrs. Childress, the librarian, drawn mostly in blue. She is a miniature human being in comparison with the great oafs, drawn in heavy black lines, who surround her in the library. Elijah had perfectly captured the woman's precarious authority over them all. He'd invested her with blue beneath black lines so that the blueness is like energy held within her. As if even in her smallness, the librarian is the finished human being, whereas the students are the doofus creatures who don't know what to do with themselves and depend on petite Mrs. Childress to bring a moment of focus to their lives. The boy drawn at the front of the line was famous for his unruly behavior in school, a boy who defied teachers and administrators but who was known to revere Mrs. Childress. Suzanne is sure that only she and Elijah ever noted the unacknowledged stature of that woman in the school, which she — Suzanne — wouldn't have known how to describe. But once Elijah had set it into a picture and allowed her to see it, she could grasp what she already knew.

There was a stretch during her senior year, however, when Elijah showed her no pictures and when he seemed not to notice her at all. The place beside him was available each morning; he no longer sat on the aisle side, pretending to save it, because by then it had been established that the place was hers. Also, he'd stopped catching her eye at any time during the bus ride or the school day. In the general chaos of her life in those days, however, the change in Elijah's behavior was barely noticeable. Occasionally Suzanne wondered whether she'd done something to anger him or hurt his feelings, but nothing came to mind. And other matters demanded her attention. She'd got caught up in applying to colleges and discussing scholarships with her guidance counselors and teachers.

One cold January day when she got on the school bus, she found the seat empty, Elijah not there. Everyone on the bus seemed to be staring at her. Elijah had never missed school. Something made Suzanne glance back at the bus driver. His eyes were on her, too, in the mirror that let him monitor what went on behind him. "His mother died," the driver said quietly. "She'd been sick a long time." Suzanne nodded but said nothing. She took her seat, and the bus driver let the clutch out and started the bus. She didn't dare scoot over to the window; even with Elijah not there, it would have been wrong to take his place. She sat with her book bag in her lap, as she did every morning when he sat beside her.

The more she thought about him, the more her face burned with shame. That his mother had died was horrible. If she'd been a friend to Elijah as he'd been to her that first morning, she'd have found out why he'd been holding himself away from her all that time. Or she'd have just known — she who had once experienced what it was like to be Elijah! Everybody else on the bus — though no one said a thing — seemed to have known. All that time he'd been sitting beside Suzanne, he'd needed her to know his mother was ill, but she'd been thinking of herself and her future and the days of freedom that lay ahead of her at college. As she noticed how quiet the other kids were, she realized that tears were falling down her cheeks and splashing onto her book bag. Embarrassed, she turned toward the window and curled around herself, as Elijah did when he worked in his notebook. And it happened to her again, that sharp blast of empathy, which was like a magic trick in which she lived in Elijah's body and mind for about twenty seconds. It made her face burn all the more.

Throughout that day in school and the ride home and in her dealings with her parents and her sisters — all of them leaving her completely alone, now that they knew she was making her escape to college within the year — she was preoccupied. Before her mother called her down for dinner, she sat in her room, trying to draw a picture that would show her embracing Elijah to comfort him in his grief. But she had no talent for drawing, and even if she could have drawn what she meant, the picture would have been wrong. She had no desire to embrace him — she simply wanted to let him know that she felt his sorrow, that she was somehow with him in his sorrow, or that she wanted to be with him. The more she studied her feeble attempt at a picture, the more confused she became about what she wanted to convey to Elijah. However, as she ate with her family — who mostly talked among themselves as if she weren't there — she reconciled herself to writing him a note. When she finished washing the dishes — the chore that had fallen to her when she was twelve by agreement among the family — she went upstairs to compose her note to him. She paced her room, she did some of her homework, she read in the library book Mrs. Childress had recommended, and she composed draft after draft of her note of condolence. No matter what she wrote, she hated the words, so she finally settled on writing the thing she hated the least, which, as it turned out, was the most impersonal version of what she wanted to say.

Dear Elijah,
    I am so sorry about your mother. Please forgive me for not having spoken to you about her before this. I know this must

be a terrible time for you, and I hope you will let me know if there is anything I can do to help make things easier for you.

Your school bus friend,
Suzanne

She had the note ready to give him the next day, but he wasn't on the bus. That was a Friday, and the funeral — she learned from the biweekly county newspaper — would be on Saturday. She considered attending — she could walk to the church — but decided it would be a mistake to make a statement like that to her family and the townspeople. She was pretty certain he would be on the bus on Monday morning, when she could discreetly pass him the note. All through the weekend, she agonized, but she always came up with the same answer: she couldn't pretend she didn't know what had happened, she couldn't draw a picture for him, and she couldn't speak to him; she had to give him the words she had written.

Monday morning Elijah was back in his seat, looking out the window. When Suzanne sat down, he didn't move. The note, in its envelope, was tucked into an outside compartment of her book bag; she'd planned exactly how to pass it to him. She waited through the next two stops, until Leonard Branscomb stepped up into the bus. Leonard was a tall, red-faced farm boy who always had funny things to say to his pals in the back of the bus. Suzanne waited until he was directly beside her, carrying on as usual and distracting everyone as he made his way to the back. That was when she said, quietly but definitely, "Elijah," a few inches from his ear. She witnessed the little jolt she'd caused him. When he turned his eyes to her, she pushed the envelope against his hand, positioned so that he could see his name on it. He took it and once more gave her a look, one that struck Suzanne as fearful. *Why should he be afraid of me?* she thought as he faced the window again, curling around himself in that way of his.

Relieved, she excused herself from worrying any further about him or what he would make of what she had written. She opened her library book and, her eyes on the page, began savoring a vision of herself walking across a campus in springtime — Radford College or maybe V.P.I. She would be wearing new clothes; she would be in the company of a boy or a friend; she would have the admiration of her professors . . .

She heard her name in a belch of sound, as if croaked by a whale or a porpoise trained to imitate human noises, and found herself staring straight at Elijah's tear-streaked face. He grasped her hand, tugging it and holding on to it. He uttered two more syllables — "Thank you" — as if he were talking through his nose, yet loud enough for the kids near them to hear. The whites of his eyes gleamed weirdly. Then, perhaps sensing that she was repulsed by his behavior, he released her hand and jerked himself back toward the window, raising the hand that had grasped hers to wipe his wet cheeks and eyes.

What she had to do was — she knew it as clearly as if it had appeared before her in letters of fire — TOUCH HIM. But what she really wanted more than anything was to move away, put some distance between his flesh and hers. Of course there was no other seat, and she probably wouldn't have moved even if there had been one. But she couldn't will herself to put a hand on his arm or shoulder or knee, couldn't force even a whispered *I'm sorry.* All she could do was sit, locked in her sitting-on-the-bus posture. The moment passed. She sensed that if she so much as brushed him with her fingers, he'd strike at her in anger. Her face blazed with shame.

She heard noise behind her and across the aisle — stifled laughter. She guessed the kids sitting there — Becky Stoots and

Mildred Coleman — were talking about what they'd just seen happen between her and Elijah. She could turn toward them and give them a look, but that would make things worse. So she sat quietly, hoping he would understand that she meant to endure the humiliation with him. But she knew he wouldn't see it that way. He'd see it correctly: she'd betrayed him. She'd written and delivered that note to make herself feel better. And when he'd responded openly, she'd pulled away from him. So if it was possible to make Elijah Limeberry's life worse — the life of a friendless boy who'd been brutally mocked from his first day of school and whose mother had just died — that was what she'd done. That was how she'd repaid his kindness in rescuing her on her first day of riding the bus.

Suzanne knows this episode is at the core of what she protects from acquaintances who want to know where she came from and what it was like to grow up in Appalachia. But this isn't all. There are probably forty or fifty old betrayals and humiliations from those days that radiate around that single moment on the bus with the Mute. Suzanne can evoke an amalgamation of smells that come from that bus, from the Colemans and Stootses and Branscombs and Mabes and Davises who got on at this stop and that one. Some of those children were clean, but few bathed regularly, and their clothes were rarely washed. One or two had the fragrance of fried side meat clinging to them. The Porter children came straight to the bus from milking cows and slopping hogs. She can probably even bring back the exact fragrance of Mildred Coleman's hair spray after she'd been caught in the rain — the memory of that scent oddly thrills Suzanne when it returns to her.

From her hundreds of mornings and afternoons on the school bus, she can bring back snapped bra straps and cruelly flipped ears and ripped shirts and thrown condoms and tampons and curses and names called and blows struck and even the time Leonard Branscomb spat in the face of Buntsy Russell and dared him to do something about it. And there was Botch Arnold pulling a sharpened beer-can opener from his sock and threatening Trenton Mabe with it; that memory is such a squalid little treasure that Suzanne knows she will never let it go. Though she has devoted most of her life to putting them behind her — to denying them — these people remain an essential part of who she is.

It isn't so much the squalor or ignorance or ugliness of her former life that Suzanne wants to conceal. She knows she's locked in this — how to name it? — *posture* of half-hearted empathy. All she had to do was despise Elijah Limeberry, the way everyone else did. He'd have understood, and she'd have caused him no pain. All she has to do now to separate herself — cleanly and completely — from her past is to despise it. But she can't.

He paid her back. When she remembers it, she grimaces. Whether or not payback was all he intended, Suzanne will never know. It was on one of her last days of school, when she was still giddy from the offer of a full scholarship from Hollins College. She'd applied there only to appease the English teacher, who was the most passionate of those urging her to get a college education. The scholarship stopped her parents' resistance to her going. They could no longer say they weren't about to pay good money for her to go off to some fancy college just to come back home and turn up her nose at them. That spring, her senior year in high school, she was strolling down a grand boulevard of possibility and opportunity. The episode of her treachery to Elijah was fading from memory, and she had only a few more days of riding the school bus before leaving it forever. She and Elijah had continued to share a seat, but they both understood it was for the sake of deflecting attention from them. If she'd sat elsewhere, their bus comrades would have teased them without mercy. So when she took her seat those last mornings, Suzanne endured the discomfort she felt emanating from Elijah, as she supposes he endured whatever feelings were coming from her — though it troubles her to name what they were. She tells herself, *Sorrow — I felt sorry for what had happened between us* — but the truth is that she loathed him. Now that she had betrayed Elijah, what she had to bear, while sitting beside him, was loathing of such intensity that she must have reeked of it, like the smell of cow manure that came onto the bus with the Porter kids.

The grimace that comes to Suzanne's face now — twenty-two years after the fact — is focused on her discomfort with that feeling. Not that she thinks loathing is an unacceptable feeling, but that she felt it for a boy in whose body and mind she actually lived for about thirty-five seconds. And for a boy whose kindness had saved her in a desperate moment.

The Mute left an envelope, with her name on it, stuck in her locker door on the last day of school. He must have been paying close attention to her and planning carefully, because it was the last time she'd ever open that locker. And she wasn't going to ride the bus home that afternoon, because she'd been invited to spend the night with a classmate who was also going to Hollins in the fall and who said she wanted to get to know Suzanne a little better. When Suzanne saw the envelope, she knew immediately who'd put it there — it was exactly like the envelope she'd passed to him on the bus, except that it had SUZANNE printed on it in black ink. She dreaded reading the note so much that she carried it into the girls' bathroom, and though there wasn't a soul there, at the end of the school day, she took the envelope into a stall before opening it.

It was a folded card of good stationery — the same as she'd used for her note to him — and when she unfolded it, she found the inside entirely inked over. While Suzanne stood in the shadowy little box with the toilet — and the smell of the girls' bathroom making her feel slightly nauseated — she saw that there was blue ink beneath the nearly solid blackness. The black pen strokes had just enough space between them for a vague blue shape to be discernible. She left the stall and carried the note to the window to study it in bright light. And still she couldn't make it out. There was something back there; she thought it was a face, but she couldn't be sure. The no-image image nagged her to study it more carefully — she thought about looking at it at home with a magnifying glass. But as she stood by the window, holding the card, something began to anger her. Something sparked in her. She ripped it! Then she ripped the two pieces into four. Those two rippings happened in an instant, and she stood holding the quartered parts. Finally, she took them, with the envelope, to the big trash can, where she tore the pieces into the size of snowflakes. As she let them fall into the can, she took special care that the SUZANNE on the envelope was so thoroughly shredded that not even a genius of a puzzle worker could have reassembled it.

That was perhaps the first time Suzanne had deliberately destroyed something. Leaving the restroom and walking out of the school building toward the parking lot to meet her classmate, she was shocked by her exhilaration. Her hands still tingled from the ripping. *That was good,* she thought. *That was just fine,* Suzanne decided as she hurried toward the girl who wanted to know her better.

II

A S A COUNSELOR at Camp Equinox, Jack came to know an angry child. Ten-year-old Colleen Davis was a sure bet to disrupt every afternoon's quiet hour in the cabins. Her file offered no explanation for Colleen's anger — her father managed a car dealership, her mother was a bank teller, she had an older brother and a younger sister, she was an above-average student in school. And she wasn't shy or ugly or overly pretty or fat or thin or possessed of any oddness of speech or physical appearance. In an evening meeting, Jack's boss, the assistant director, told the counselors that he'd made a phone call to Colleen's parents and that the mother seemed genuinely surprised to hear that her daughter woke up mad and stayed mad throughout her day at camp. "She's not like that at home," the mother insisted. But she agreed that if Colleen didn't change her ways, she would drive up to Vermont and take her daughter home.

The child had springy hair, a head full of ringlets that by midsummer were sun-lightened to a reddish copper. Except for the set of her jaw and the tight lines of her mouth, she'd have been a charmer. Master at using an elbow, a hip, or a shoulder to bump another kid, she was also good at pinching, though never with enough force to cause an outright fight. She wore just enough of a devilish grin to suggest that she was teasing. Kids complained or shoved her back or yelled at her, and they often told on her, but they didn't seem to hate her. On the contrary, they often played up to her and gave the appearance of liking her and wanting to improve her mood. Colleen would have none of it; she used her raspy mean-kid voice to call them "little frog face" or "dog mouth." A boy or girl cozying up to her was likely to be elbowed hard enough to bring tears.

She reminded Jack of his cranky Grandmother Nelson, who only occasionally allowed a friend or relative to jolly her into a good mood. Something about Colleen suggested that she, too, was ready to be jollied, though most of the counselors quickly got fed up with her meanness and gave her time-outs to separate her from the other kids. And from themselves — because Colleen was a subversive presence around the counselors.

By the swimming pool one afternoon, Jack watched Colleen devil a boy named Chris. He was bigger than Colleen, though not nearly the swimmer she was. Evidently Colleen enjoyed having him at this disadvantage. Less evidently — as Jack observed in her face when the boy wasn't looking at her — she liked Chris. On this particular day, she appeared more likely to drown the boy than to win his affection. She lured him into following her to the deep end and then managed to push him under and hold him there long enough to frighten him. When Chris finally made his way to the edge of the pool, sputtering and gasping, Jack stepped near where Colleen was treading water. He was on his free time at the moment, but he couldn't let the situation continue. He knelt by the poolside, and said, so firmly that he surprised himself, "Colleen, I'd like you to come over and sit beside me for a while."

This was an unusual step. Counselors sent Colleen away; they didn't ask her to come closer. Other kids — after Colleen had administered some punishment to them — tried to send her away. Chris gave Jack a look of gratitude for removing the devil-girl from the pool. Or maybe the look was simply one of delight at seeing her receive some punishment. The other kids generally liked it when Colleen was punished, because she put on a show of being tough.

"Over here, please. Let's sit down." Jack directed her to a picnic table in the shade. Out of the pool, in her green one-piece, Colleen looked small; she probably weighed no more than seventy-five pounds. Two kids moved away from the table when they saw Jack meant to use it as a time-out station for her. Jack sat down first, in a relaxed posture, his back to the tabletop, and facing the pool, which, from this distance, was a circus of chaos. He leaned back and rested his elbows behind him. Colleen sat on the bench as far away as she could, but Jack asked her to scoot a little closer so that they could talk. She did, but she turned her body away from him; he suspected she was making pouty faces.

"You're a good swimmer, Colleen. You must have started taking lessons when you were really little."

He didn't expect an answer. She turned her head to stare at him. So this was going to be her strategy. But since she wasn't making faces, he decided not to object. To ease his discomfort, he went on talking. "You ever see anybody drown, Colleen? Or see a drowned person? I did one time. The summer after I was in fifth grade, a couple of my classmates went out in a boat with some big boys. They capsized the boat, and my classmates weren't wearing life jackets, and they had all their clothes on. They knew how to swim, but their clothes dragged them down, and they couldn't make it to shore. Their names were Joe and

Charles. I saw those boys when the rescue squad pulled them out of the river. Their faces were blue. I saw both of them. And I'll tell you this, Colleen: I don't ever want to see another drowned person."

Jack's voice was shaky by the time he finished telling the story. He was seventeen years old, and this was his first real job; he'd had no experience in trying to correct anyone's behavior, and the situation with Colleen seemed to him precarious. He'd read about those boys' drowning in a book of short stories for his English class at Choate, but since he knew that Colleen wouldn't listen to him if he told her something he'd read in a book, he'd pretended to have been right there on the riverbank, watching. Now he was surprised at the emotion that welled up in him — as if he'd actually seen the blue faces of his fifth-grade classmates.

The girl continued to study Jack's face. He studied hers, too, and let the silence extend far beyond what he thought was reasonable. The sun had darkened her skin, especially across the bridge of her nose and her cheekbones. She really was a child — though now that he saw the childish quality of her features, he wondered why he and the other counselors hadn't been more aware of it. This girl wasn't all that far past babyhood — or at least toddlerhood. Her pupils were such a deep brown, they startled Jack into thinking she knew he had lied to her about the drowned boys.

"Feel this," she told him quietly. She stepped forward, took Jack's right hand, grasped the first two fingers, and pushed them into the mass of curls on the left side of her head, just above her ear.

Jack could feel nothing beyond what he took to be the ordinary surface of a child's scalp. But Colleen was watching him so gravely that he carefully felt around the whole area with his fingertips. And as he did, he began to sense an irregularity, a curve of the bone beneath the skin. It shot a little jolt of fear in him, but in as quiet a voice as she had used, he asked, "Does it hurt?"

Colleen nodded. "I can't sleep on that side."

"Does your mother know about it?"

"No."

"Who does know about it?"

Colleen shook her head.

As Jack studied her, he received small pieces of how it must have been for her this summer at Equinox. She hadn't told her parents about her head, because they would have taken her to the doctor, who would have told them to keep her at home. After she got here, and her head had started really bothering her, she got more and more scared. Then she wanted to tell somebody, but didn't know who. Today — just now — she'd chosen him. Suddenly he wanted to pick the child up and run with her to the infirmary, but he knew that if he did she would hate him.

"Let's go see the nurse, Colleen. She'll be interested in that part of your head, and she'll know what to do about it. Okay?"

Colleen nodded and took the hand he extended. That's what got to Jack — she held on to his hand all the way to the infirmary, a good ten-minute walk from the swimming pool.

Later, as Jack remembered it, his stroll with Colleen to the camp infirmary lasted many minutes. He let the child set the pace, and she took it slowly. The path was through a patch of woods that on this summer day was cool and fragrant. "Will they make me go home?" she asked. Jack told her he thought the nurse would probably call her parents to discuss with them what they should do. He said her parents might want to take her to a doctor back home. "That's what I thought," Colleen said. Her voice had taken on the edge of anger the counselors had been hearing over the past weeks, and her hand was pulling down on Jack's. But he was glad she didn't let go.

"You'll be glad to see your parents, won't you?"

When she didn't answer, he figured she was going to ignore the question. Finally, when she did speak, there was no more anger in her voice. "I like it here," she said.

In those words — which were the last of their conversation — Jack heard, or imagined, a fear and sorrow he wouldn't have thought a child capable of expressing. He started to say something like "I don't blame you," or "Yes, it's pretty nice here." But the air was woodsy, the sun streamed down through the leaves in patterns of light and shadow all around them — so he realized he didn't need to say anything. He didn't even squeeze her hand, though he was tempted to. He did, however, sneak a look to try to see her face. She kept it turned away, so all he saw was the head of copper-tinted curls that for the rest of his life would stand for the girl named Colleen Davis whom he had known the summer he was seventeen.

After he walked with her inside the infirmary to the nurse, events took place quickly. By dinnertime Colleen's mother had arrived at Equinox, and just before dark, Jack, with almost everyone else at the camp, was standing in the parking lot, waving goodbye to a face behind a car window.

During the last weeks of his job at Equinox, Jack was incidentally informed of Colleen Davis's medical progress. Doctors in her New York town sent her to Albany, and those doctors dispatched her to the Children's Hospital in Boston. After surgery and radiation treatment, the Boston doctors expected Colleen to be fine; the chances were excellent for a complete recovery. This news didn't affect Jack as deeply as he wanted it to. He went for a walk by himself and tried to imagine her, anesthetized and lying on her side on a table under bright lights, a tray of instruments, doctors and nurses in their caps and masks clustered around her. There had to be some correspondence between what he knew Colleen was going through and the intensity of their walk together through the woods from the pool to the infirmary. But he couldn't feel it, couldn't bring it into focus in his mind.

His first evening back home in New York City, Jack told his parents about Colleen. Ordinarily he wouldn't have done such a thing, but he hadn't seen his mother and father for many weeks, and the usual silence of their dinners suddenly was burdensome and unnecessary. Sitting with them at the dining room table, he understood that because of what had happened with Colleen, he'd grown up. "There was this kid at camp, a girl —" he began. "Colleen. She was a really bad kid."

Jack noticed that his monologue startled his parents. High-ceilinged and shadowy, the dining room was always a degree or two cooler than the rest of the apartment. From early in his childhood, he'd understood that he was to be on his best behavior here. A monumental silver tea service occupied the top of one side table, and an engraved chafing dish on a silver tray sat atop another. The paintings on the walls were ones his father especially valued, and the table had been designed according to his father's specifications. Guests became quiet when they stepped into this room. Conversations were almost always held in murmurs. "Our dinner parties are intimate occasions," his mother liked to say. Now, while Jack's reedy voice fluttered up into the space around the chandelier — "she put my fingers right up against the side of her head" — his parents eyed him as if they knew their son was about to confess to something awful he'd done at camp. He thought they'd be relieved that the end of his story was nothing to bring them trouble or disgrace, that what he was offering them was *philosophy* — a story about life and death.

As Jack spoke, his father slipped his appointment notebook and his pen out of his jacket pocket. He didn't make a show of it, but he wasn't trying to be subtle either. Jack went on speaking, because his father gave no sign of wanting him to stop. After his father opened the notebook and carefully wrote something in it, his eyes went back to Jack and he listened a while longer. Then he wrote down something else, and Jack was thrilled. He spoke with greater confidence, since he'd never experienced this level of attention from his father. Goosebumps rose on his arms as he made his way to the end of the tale.

"I probably won't see her again, but that's not what's important. She told me the secret she'd been keeping to herself. I don't think she'd have done that if I hadn't said the right things to her. So no matter what happens from here on out, it's as if I gave her something, and she gave me something in return."

When he stopped talking, the silence of the dining room hovered over him and his parents and the china and glasses and candelabra and silverware. He made himself pick up his fork and take a mouthful of rice, but it was so cold that it was hard to swallow. He set the fork on his place with an audible clink; his parents had stopped eating, too. Each seemed to be waiting for the other to pick up the conversation. Jack's father put his notebook and pen back in his pocket and cleared his throat. "Very commendable, son," he said.

"We're proud of you, Jack," his mother murmured.

"Thank you." Jack looked from one to the other. He knew his parents had said the right things — and that he, too, had said what was proper. But if his father had risen from the table and cursed him, Jack couldn't have felt worse. He felt pain when he knew he should have been taking pleasure from his parents' understanding and appreciation; that's when he understood that something was grossly wrong with him. Days later, that sense of something wrong inside kept him from doing what he wanted: to sneak a look at his father's appointment book. For years afterward, Jack remained curious about the words in the notebook.

During his senior year at Choate, Jack lost track of Colleen. He could have got in touch with her family — he had her parents' address and phone number from the file at camp. But he didn't, though he wasn't sure why. He felt guilty for not making the effort. Often enough, he thought of the day she gave him that level gaze, quietly told him, "Feel this," and moved his hand to the side of her head. He felt guilty about savoring the memory. It was a terrible thing that Colleen had had to go through; he reminded himself of her suffering. When it came time to apply for a summer job, he hesitated about writing to Mrs. Rothwell, the camp director, to let her know that he wanted to come back. But after it was almost too late, he did, more out of reluctance to look for a new job than from his wish to return to Equinox.

If another counselor hadn't pointed her out, Jack wouldn't have recognized Colleen. The curls were gone. Instead, there was a veritable pelt of short, shiny, dark brown hair, and the child who wore it was radiantly pale. That child was also one of the happiest Jack had ever seen. In her body movements and speech, she was evidently slower than the other children; her facial expression, however, was not so much a smile as a look of constant good cheer. Soon after her arrival, the other campers surrounded her, as if they sought nourishment from the spirit of this pale one among them. Counselors, too, were drawn to the child, eager to be of assistance to her, or maybe just wanting to be near her beaming face.

Jack found himself avoiding the sight of the new Colleen and everyone flocking around her. Even on her first day at camp, he was angered by the whole show of that child and the people vying for her attention. There was nothing insincere about her manner or attitude; nevertheless, she upset him — or the fact of her upset him. That night in his bunk, unable to sleep, Jack figured it out. This saintly child had replaced the old Colleen. He missed the bad-tempered, bad-behaving, sharp-elbowed, springy-haired, alert hellion who was the old Colleen. That one wasn't ever coming back.

At the softball game a couple of weeks after the start of camp, Jack became aware that Colleen was studying him. By now the other campers had become used to her; some had grown a little impatient with her slow speech and body movements. Everyone was still warmly solicitous of her, but now, more often than not, she was encouraged to sit and watch a softball or volleyball game rather than to join in. To everyone's relief the child's spirits apparently weren't dampened, nor did she seem to mind being off by herself. At the moment, she was sitting alone on the grass in a shady place, a huge old ash tree beside the softball field, but Jack knew that circumstance was temporary. During the course of the game, players from both teams drifted in and out of the shade. It was Saturday afternoon, a time when a few parents came to visit and perhaps take their camper out for a meal or a tourist excursion. The softball game was the only activity on the schedule after lunch on Saturday, and nobody took it seriously; it was just a pleasant way to pass the time.

Jack had set up a folding chair a couple of yards off to the side of first base. From that vantage point he could serve as coach, umpire, or cheerleader, whatever the situation called for. Today he was wearing shorts and had taken off his T-shirt. What he was really doing was working on his tan, but he also enjoyed the detachment this role allotted him during the softball games. Occasionally he'd be called on to pinch-hit or take somebody's place in the field for an inning or two, but mostly he was able to sit in a trance, feeling the breeze on his skin and soaking up the sunlight. However, for some moments now, a mild disturbance had interfered with his reverie. Colleen was visible only if he looked toward her, but he felt her attention focused on him. He'd expected her to approach him, but he couldn't relax, with her watching him.

He stood up and stretched and continued watching the soft-ball players as he slipped on his T-shirt. He dawdled because he didn't want to appear too purposeful. Not only did he want to avoid causing Colleen anxiety, he also didn't want to draw attention. Almost nobody at camp this year seemed to remember that he'd been the one last summer to discover there was something wrong with her. Also, nobody seemed to have noticed that this summer he and Colleen had not spoken to each other. Now that he knew what he was going to do, he could feel his heart thumping. He shoved his hands into the pockets of his shorts and stepped over to Colleen, trying to look friendly and casual.

She was sitting in that peculiar way girls sometimes do, sort of on her hip, her knees bent and her legs to the side. Her smile suggested that she, too, was hoping for a chance to talk.

"Hi, Colleen." Once he entered the shade, he let himself down on the grass beside her. This way they both could observe the softball players, which ought to make it easier for them to say what they had to say to each other. "I'm glad you came back this summer," he began. He was aware that he was excited, but he was sure he'd relax in a moment. From having seen her with the other children, he knew that Colleen was slow to answer questions; you had to wait for her to find the right words, and sometimes that took a while. So he was careful not to put her on the spot. After he got himself to start speaking, he kept going, so as not to inflict on her the awkwardness of having to re-spond.

In his monologue, he told the girl he'd thought about her a great deal during the past year and that he'd been worried about her, even though he hadn't sent her any letters or cards. And the main reason he hadn't done those things was that he had this silly idea that he should pretend she'd be fine, as if there was nothing wrong with her, and then, if he did that, there really would be nothing wrong with her, and she would be fine, even though he knew how silly the idea was. Why, just look at her right here and now, absolutely fine; so he'd been right after all; he'd done the right thing, because now they had this pretty weather, this great afternoon, and all the rest of the summer to enjoy camp, and he remembered how she'd said she liked it here, and now she was back . . .

He hadn't looked at her for a while, but as he went on and became more anxious about the impression he was making and how to wrap this whole thing up, he cast quick glances in her direction. That's how he noticed that her lips were moving. She continued, as he did, to watch the softball players, and her lip movements were slight, but as his talking accelerated, he saw that she was shaping words, slowly and carefully, even though he couldn't hear them. Of course he wanted to know what she had to say — that was why he'd come over here in the first place — so he brought himself to a midsentence halt and leaned to-ward her. At first he couldn't make out what she was saying. Then he realized that she was whispering one syllable at a time, with a three- or four-second pause after each. Hoping no one would notice, he leaned still closer.

" — want — you — to — go — away — I —"

It was as if someone had hooked wires into his ears and shot electricity into them. He wanted to jump up and run — but didn't want to make a scene. So he sat still, leaning away from Colleen and watching her, as if he were thinking about something she'd told him. With her eyes following the ball players, she continued to move her lips, as if repeating a secret to herself. When Jack stood up, he had an urge to shove her with his knee; he could imagine it vividly enough almost to feel the satisfaction of doing it. Instead, he brushed off the seat of his shorts and, with exaggerated politeness, spoke to the top of the child's head, "Goodbye, Colleen. I hope you'll feel better soon." Then he walked back to his chair beside first base and forced himself to sit there until he was certain Colleen had left her place under the shady tree.

III

SUZANNE CAN'T STAND the way Jack plays to people. She remembers when Jack didn't feel he had to be Mr. Personality. He was himself and plenty charming enough for her. But nowadays he belly-laughs; he *ha*'s and *ho*'s and *huh*'s; he grins like a jack-o'-lantern; he repeats what the other person said; and it's all one big show. It's because of his job, but she's sick of it — sick of him. She listens hard, trying to catch one thoughtful sentence, but he has yet to utter it. The worst is that she's aware of how he performs for *her*, even when he brings her the newspaper and her coffee in the morning. "Here you are, my darling," he sings out as if they're in a musical comedy. She pretends she's too sleepy to say thank you. She hopes this acute alertness to him is a phase she's passing through and that in a few weeks she'll stop bridling at her husband's artificiality. Maybe it'll stop bothering her like a fever blister, like an earache, like a bad memory.

She reminds herself that Jack is basically an okay human being. She puts it to herself — "basically an okay human being" — because he's definitely got his faults. Selling him to a new wife would be a problem. The idea amuses her. "Once or twice a year Jack will lie to you, and he'll probably accidentally humiliate you in public about every three or four months. But basically he's an okay human being."

Their latest venture is getting a dog, a yellow lab named Sam. "Dog or a divorce," Jack tells everyone. "It had to be one or the other." Then he gives his belly laugh. At such moments Suzanne could kill him. Though he says this to play to the person he's talking to — the same way he tries to show off Sam's "tricks," which are sitting down, shaking paws, and chasing a tennis ball — he obviously doesn't recognize how accurate he is. He doesn't know she went to a lawyer last year to talk "in a general way" about the implications of divorce. If he knew, he wouldn't be throwing the *d*-word around for the amusement of their neighbors and friends.

Sam's puppyhood, now over, rescued their marriage — at least temporarily. That's how Suzanne puts it to herself. Sam was irresistible as a puppy, so awkward, affectionate, and funny. What Suzanne acknowledges, to her discomfort, is that having the dog brings her pleasure only because she's with Jack. By herself she wouldn't want Sam. After the third time she had to clean up his poop, she'd have taken him back to the lady who sold him to them. Not that she doesn't clean up after him, but at least the task doesn't fall to her every time. Jack takes his turn. And — she has to admit — her pleasure in the cute things about Sam is increased by Jack's witnessing them, too.

"Here you go, my darling," Jack says as he approaches the bed in the dark. "Your coffee, your paper" — he pauses while he puts the paper beside her, turns on the light, and sets her coffee cup on the night table — "and your dog!" He sings it out like the tenor in an opera. For this time of morning — six-thirty — he's outrageously loud. He pats the side of the bed where he'd been sleeping an hour ago, and Sam jumps up, pushes his snout toward Suzanne, and sticks out his tongue. "That's right. Give your mommy a kiss," Jack says. He knows Suzanne hates Sam to lick her face. Smiling, he watches the two of them and then walks out of the room. Finally she can relax and read the paper, with Sam settling down beside her.

One of Jack's saving graces is that he's a workaholic. In another half-hour, he'll leave the house and walk to his office downtown. He doesn't spend a lot of time hanging around Suzanne; he gives her breathing space, though she knows that's not how he thinks of it. Suzanne, always inclined to lose herself in her research, is finding that middle age gives her more patience to concentrate on her work. She can walk into her study with the intention of spending a quick hour looking at slides and reading, and then find that the entire afternoon has passed. "Earth to Suzanne," Jack will call as he knocks on her door at dinnertime. "Earth to Suzanne! Is there human life in that spaceship?"

This "protected" aspect of her life is Suzanne's main reservation about divorcing Jack. What other partner would give her the time she needs, not only for her career but for her spiritual well-being? Jack believes his great virtue as a husband is that he brings her coffee and the newspaper in the morning and cooks dinner most evenings. She assumes that he does these things because his father would have never dreamed of doing them. He's constantly reminding her that, in spite of his demanding job, he does carry out these tasks. Not that she'd miss the "favors" if he stopped tomorrow. He doesn't understand that the most valuable deed he performs is leaving her alone. And though most of his conversation with her is of trivial content, at least he "stays out of her head," as she puts it to herself. He doesn't snoop into her personal or professional life; he doesn't pester her to spend more time with him; he doesn't, like some husbands she knows, want to know where his wife is at all times. Now, if she could stop being irritated by his superficiality, Suzanne could be relatively happy.

"Pat, Jack," she hears him braying into the downstairs phone. "Just thought I'd leave you a message to remind you we've got a four-thirty match this afternoon at the club. Get ready for a butt-kicking, pal. See you on the court."

Suzanne sets aside the newspaper when she realizes she hasn't been reading the page directly in front of her. Lately, she's been planning to write an article on the last years of Georges de La Tour, on the apparent contradiction between the deeply humane vision of his paintings and the recently documented nastiness of his character. Court records show that around 1650, the painter, who seemed to cherish the resourcefulness of the poor, beat a peasant nearly to death. When she came across that bit of information in a journal, Suzanne brooded over it for a long while — it touched something in her, though she couldn't have said what. But the revelation of La Tour's savagery also appealed to her because one of her "scholarly interests" is the impulse of a culture to sentimentalize its art and its artists. She's already begun to formulate her "challenging readings" of *The Fortune Teller* and *The Musicians' Brawl*. And to anticipate the outraged responses she's likely to receive. "The strident feminist vision of Professor Suzanne Nelson once again leads her to denigrate some of the most beloved . . ."

"La Tour was an old fart," Suzanne whispers to Sam, who's lying on his side, sleeping soundly. "What little humanity he had was in his eye and his hand, not in his mind or his heart." Having thought about the phrasing for some days, she wanted to try the sentence out loud. Now, having said it, today she may put it into her computer and eventually look at the observation as printing on paper. The image in her mind is of the old painter striding into Lunéville, turning a fierce face toward any beggar who dares look at him too long.

Sam stirs. Suzanne envies the dog's ability to slide into sleep so quickly and easily — as if sleep were his natural state, his true self. Lying flat beside her, snoring and breathing ponderously, Sam seems to be in a great canyon of dreams. Suzanne finds something portentous in Jack's being her living alarm clock. Almost always she's awakened by Jack — though, she must admit, always considerately. Nevertheless, she loves sleeping and dreaming so much, it's as if Jack is stealing her pleasures.

She considers picking up the newspaper again, but she continues to stare at the ceiling, happily setting her mind on old La Tour, rich and famous in his late fifties (though in Suzanne's mind he appears white-haired, wrinkled, and enfeebled by arthritis). The only painter in Lunéville, he lives like royalty. The esteem granted him by the common people stems from their belief that he is religiously gifted, because of pictures like *The Magdalen at the Mirror* and *Newborn Child*. Suzanne is as certain as if La Tour himself had confessed it to her that, when he was around forty, he discovered a technique for using light to convey spirituality, to make his work appear divinely inspired. Suzanne can imagine the devious smile on his face when he sees what he's going to be able to accomplish. "It must have come to him in his studio one day that he was going to be a rich man. All he had to do was use his little trick. Tell the same lie again and again," she murmurs to the dog sleeping beside her. The next thought that comes to her is so startling that she sits up straight and says it aloud: "That's what Jack does!"

Jack is alone in his office, working at his keyboard, when he hears a light tapping at his closed door. He looks up from his computer screen, quickly checks his watch — it's seven-thirty A.M., an hour before anyone else is supposed to show up. Jack is generally acknowledged to be the public-relations genius of the state of Vermont, as well as the main man of this firm. It is understood that he is not to be disturbed until after nine. "What the hell?" he murmurs, distracted, but he goes to the door. Somewhat irritated, he opens it.

Smiling at him, rosy-cheeked, fragrant, in a yellow sheath dress with a flowered black scarf, her shoulders back, her chin up, her hair shockingly chopped into an ultra-continental look, is Elly Jacobs.

Jack steps back and gapes. Five years ago, when her hair was shoulder length, they were lovers. Their affair ended badly. Suzanne found out about it; Elly left town, having won a fellowship to study primitive religious art for a year at the American Academy of Rome; and Jack fell into a mild but long-term depression. He's not much given to fantasy, but as Elly stands here before him, he feels as if, out of a deep well of wishfulness, he has constructed this moment.

They stand where they are, saying nothing, desire building in him. He thinks it may be building in her, too.

He clears his throat.

Elly steps forward.

Then they're embracing and kissing, both of them close to crying. Jack's got an erection that's prehistoric in its urgency.

"Where are you staying?" he rasps out, and Elly whispers, "The Radisson."

"Let's go," he says.

In less than four minutes they're out of Jack's office, out of the building, and beside each other, stepping crisply down the blocks toward the lakefront and the hotel. It's not yet eight. At not many minutes after eight, they're naked and under the covers of the huge bed in Elly's seventh-floor room. She comes quickly, so he lets himself go, too; then they both have a little crying to do in each other's arms. Finally, turning on his back, he says, "I guess we'd better talk, hadn't we?"

Elly sits up, plumps the pillows the way she likes them, and leans back. Jack watches her breasts while she does these things.

"If you want to," she says, turning and smiling at him. "Sure. We can do that."

Surrounded by his dogs, La Tour walks from his estate into town. His canine entourage kicks up as much dust as a coach and horses. La Tour could ride in his carriage, but today he walks to let the town see how vigorous he is. For this outing he has had himself elaborately bathed and dressed and has selected his newest wig. Now he converses with the dogs, calling them by name. Caravaggio, the smallest and ugliest, is the one he most favors. La Tour knows the townspeople hate his dogs, which is all the more reason for him to fawn over them in public. His dogs eat better than most of the poor in Lunéville. La Tour knows that his contempt for the poor makes no sense; as a child, he had lived through many a day when he would have stolen food from a dog could he have done so. No matter; he despises those people all the more because he knows their lives so intimately.

La Tour's errand is to go to the shoemaker's, but not for shoes. He intends to ask Lavalette to send his daughter to pose for him. There will be a discussion of money, to which La Tour looks forward. He can afford to pay the shoemaker a handsome wage for the daughter's services, but he won't pay a penny more than he must. Of course La Tour wants to see the girl, Vivienne — she's fifteen — but he suspects that most of his pleasure today will be in bargaining with her father. The man will be torn between greed and protectiveness. La Tour is almost certain how the negotiations will turn out. He will explain to the father that the girl will be asked to pose without her clothes but that no harm will come to her, because he is, after all, an old man. The father will proclaim that no amount of money could persuade him to send his daughter to pose without her clothes in La Tour's studio. La Tour will say that he understands, that he couldn't afford to pay more than such-and-such an amount anyway. The father will clear his throat, stare out a window for a moment, then ask how long the painter would expect to keep his model at the studio. The daughter is needed to work at the shop in the afternoons. For long minutes La Tour will needle Lavalette, making it clear, without actually saying so, that he understands him to be a person of no integrity whatsoever. La Tour will scale down the original amount he suggested but will keep it high enough to prevent the shoemaker from refusing him. In short, he will make Lavalette as miserable as possible.

La Tour plans, when they have come to an agreement, to stage a humiliating little drama. He will call the shoemaker and his wife and daughter outside and introduce them to Caravaggio. After making the unattractive dog sit up for them, he will force the family to laugh at the trick. And then he will touch the daughter's cheek, look penetratingly into her eyes, and say that he expects her at his studio promptly at ten tomorrow morning. The only thing that will spoil this episode for La Tour is that his shoulder will catch fire the next morning when he tries to maneuver a brush. He hasn't been able to create a decent picture for so many years that he no longer tries. He won't be able to paint the girl. But without the burden of having to paint her, perhaps he'll enjoy looking at her all the more; that is what he hopes. Of course he'll have to do some acting with his palette and the canvas and the brushes before he steps over to show Vivienne exactly how he wants her to lie back on the pillows.

*

The penalty for ecstasy is severe. Five years ago that's what Jack decided when his affair with Elly ended. It hurt to be severed from her. It wasn't so much that Elly had given him ecstasy; rather, as his time with Elly moved deeper into his memory, it became more rhapsodic. To steal a few hours of sex here and there during the week, he and Elly had done a lot of sneaking around. But that wasn't how Jack remembered it. Or maybe it was how he remembered it, but it wasn't how he felt about it. And now Elly's having come back makes him feel as if he's stolen into the Garden of Eden after having been kicked out those years ago. God — Elly is here in bed with him! He touches her cheek. He moves his head down and flicks his tongue lightly at the tip of her nipple until Elly squirms and laughs and pulls his head close against her chest.

For Suzanne, today's a teaching day, so she's set aside her thoughts about La Tour for a while. She's come to understand that such mental juggling is not necessarily a bad thing. La Tour won't go away, she tells herself as she watches Sam conduct his necessaries in the back yard.

Suzanne knows she isn't a natural teacher; she's almost never at ease with the undergraduates at the University of Vermont. They're loud, aggressive, insensitive, culturally unaware, and hilariously ignorant of history in general and the visual arts in particular. "What's frightening about them," she once told Jack, "is that they have no idea how much they don't know." After she'd said it, though, she felt terrible, because she realized the same observation applied to him. Jack must have known what she was thinking, because he shrugged and grinned. "I guess," she went on, "the really frightening thing about them is that they're all pretty decent kids. Most of them know their parents have spoiled them and they don't deserve all these clothes and skis and cars and stereos and free time and access to booze and drugs. They feel a little guilty about it."

Jack's steady look made her understand that he didn't want to talk about UVM students. He was still trying to swallow the bitter pill of not being able to father his own children. Suzanne remembers that time as one of great relief over not having to raise babies — though she guesses that having her own might have made her more comfortable with the nineteen- and twenty-year-old babies who sit in her classrooms. She thinks of the boy, wearing a backward baseball cap, who, when she invited questions at the end of a lecture, raised his hand and said, in a voice that wasn't at all snotty, "Ms. Nelson, I don't understand what I'm supposed to get out of looking at this picture Rembrandt painted of himself. I don't mind these interesting pictures you show us, like the raft of the whatchamacallit and the one about the beggars fighting with each other — I mean, you can kind of make up stories to go with those paintings. But we're supposed to look at some old man just sitting there and get something out of it? It's not happening for me."

"Here, Sam," she says. "Come on, boy." The dog stops sniffing the pachysandra at the far corner of the yard and trots toward her. It astonishes her that he obeys, since by now he must know that she's about to lock him in the house, where he'll be alone for the next six hours. If she were Sam, she'd say, "See you later, boss," and trot out to the street in search of adventure. Momentarily, she's fascinated by what it is that keeps Sam from doing whatever he wants to.

Jack lies beside Elly. They've been dozing. Jack's awake now. It suddenly interests him, the act of two people falling asleep beside each other. That's really an intimate act, yet when they do it, they might as well be on opposite sides of the planet. Elly's lying on her side, away from him. Without moving, all Jack can see of her is her ever-so-short hair, a little of her neck, her shoulder, and the back of her arm down to her elbow. He lifts his head slightly and can see the side of her face, the curve of her jaw, and the rest of her arm. *That's a lovely forearm,* he thinks. "I love your forearm," he considers telling Elly when she wakes. Then he knows that now that he's awake, he wants her to be awake, too. *How ridiculous,* he tells himself. *How childish.* It hits him — suddenly. He's lonely. Right here in bed with the lover he's been yearning for these past five years, with their bodies touching under the covers, with the likelihood that they'll have sex again before Jack goes back to his office — and he's lonely! He wishes he found it amusing, but he's frightened. He's tempted to sneak out of bed, get dressed, and slip out of the room. He gets a quick glimpse of himself striding up the street, trying to look as if he'd just stepped out for coffee. The image isn't at all appealing. He nestles closer to Elly, circling his arm around her shoulder, slightly jostling her. He's not trying to wake her up, but if she does wake, it'll be all right with him.

La Tour ushers Vivienne into his studio. He discerns that she's put on a sugary scent for the occasion, but she hasn't bathed adequately — the season is not yet warm enough for people to go to the river, which is where the poor cleanse themselves before church holidays. La Tour likes neither the fragrance she's put on nor the other redolence, the one her body has generated over the days of winter and early spring. He does, however, now that she's taken off her coat, like Vivienne's neck, which is unusually long, especially long, he thinks, for a girl of her low breeding. She's put up her hair so that her neck appears shamelessly exposed. It occurs to him that she expects him to seduce her.

"Let me see your hands, my dear," he murmurs, as he directs her toward the sofa-like platform at the center of the room.

When she presents them to him, blushing, he takes them in his own and examines her palms before he turns them over. Her fingers, too, are long, and her nails are clean, but the flesh of the girl's hands is discolored — perhaps permanently — from the stains and oils of her father's shop.

"I can read and write," she says softly, lifting her eyes to meet his.

La Tour raises his eyebrows. He hadn't wondered about these abilities, but now that she has told him, his interest is piqued. "How did you learn?" he asks.

"My mother," Vivienne says. "She knows."

La Tour, who himself has no great talent when it comes to the written language, has a grudging regard for those who have.

"My mother," Vivienne says, the pride evident in her voice, "went to school." And in so doing, she informs the old painter, without intending to, that her mother married beneath herself, probably because the shoemaker had made her pregnant.

"Charming." La Tour releases Vivienne's hands and walks slowly to his easel, the station where for so many years he astonished himself with the pictures he painted — pictures he began to understand only months after he had completed them. "So your mother grew up somewhere else?" he asks.

"Paris," Vivienne whispers, with a little smile.

La Tour looks at her. The girl's expression is a little treasure. As clearly as if she had said it aloud, her face tells him she is lying. Softly he asks, "Would you like to go to Paris, Vivienne?"

Vivienne looks down, and she blushes. Her mouth opens, then closes. Apparently she doesn't trust herself to speak. She nods, but it is perhaps the most passionate nod the old painter has ever seen.

*

Suzanne enters her classroom. Given the anxiety it causes her — when she leaves school on Thursday, she begins dreading her Tuesday class — she's always surprised by how comfortable she is in the act of teaching. Today the kids are in coffin mode. Sixty pairs of vacant eyes regard her as if, try as she may to bring their owners back to life, they prefer to remain lifeless for the duration of the class.

The kids, of course, are twenty-year-olds. Suzanne understands that, rather than conveying knowledge to them, her true pedagogical responsibility is to address them, class after class, as if they were mature, perceptive, thoughtful, and observant adults. Pretend, relentlessly, that that's what they are, and maybe that's what they'll become. She suspects that her contribution to their development would be just as effective if they napped while she yammered away about the influence of Caravaggio, seventeenth-century fresco technique, the origins of Cubism, and so on. Their parents shell out $25,000 a year for them to sit in classrooms where she and her colleagues lecture to them a few hours each week. Suzanne suspects that if she thought too much about that, she'd be too terrified to utter a word. She clears her throat.

"Today we're going to look at some of the work of a painter who was famous in his day, but who, soon after his death, was almost completely forgotten. Only in the last sixty years have we begun to understand the accomplishment of this man we now consider a giant of the seventeenth century — Georges de La Tour. A basic question we have to ask ourselves when considering his paintings is how to arrive at our conclusions about artistic achievement. If La Tour was the genius we now say he was, why was his name nearly erased from our records? For a number of years, his major paintings were attributed to other artists. Today we assume we know the truth of the matter. We have 'recovered' La Tour, we like to say. But is our truth any more to be trusted than the truth of 1742 or the truth of 1850 or the truth of 1901? Should we think of the history of art in terms of 'permanent truth'?"

Suzanne pauses for a moment. Her students stare at her as if she has been speaking in tongues and they are embarrassed for her. But she's used to them. She darkens the room, sends up the first slide to the screen — La Tour's hurdy-gurdy player — and goes on with her lecture.

"Please note the paper stuffed underneath the strings of the instrument. Not only does such a detail enhance the verisimilitude of the subject, but it also testifies to the painter's respect for the beggar-musician . . ."

Jack and Elly have a room-service breakfast. They sit at a round table with a crisply starched tablecloth and white linen napkins, heavy silverware, crystal glasses, and fine china. They're nearly finished eating their fruit salad and yogurt; neither has touched the basket of muffins and croissants. They're not eating much, but the occasion has placed them together at this little table. Their intention, as Jack understands it, is to converse, but so far they haven't done so. Jack has put his tie on; his jacket lies on the chair across the room, exactly where he flung it a couple of hours ago when they burst into the room. Now he takes a deep breath and sets down his coffee cup. "You've come back," he says.

Elly nods and smiles, somewhat ruefully, he thinks. She's wearing a robe of such heavy and intricately patterned, dark blue material that it looks ecclesiastical.

"You wish you hadn't?"

Elly shakes her head and reaches across the table to touch one finger to the back of his hand. "I'm glad I came back," she says. "I just don't know what comes next."

Jack doesn't flinch from her staring. Her expression is one of careful scrutiny, but it has in it a vulnerability that is not the Elly of old. The old Elly would have been searching out his weakness — of which, Jack knows, there is plenty to be found — but this new Elly seems to be looking for strength. He doubts she'll find it. "Is staying here an option?" he asks.

"Staying here is an option," she answers softly.

"Depending on . . . ?"

"Depending on" — she doesn't say the word aloud but shapes it with her mouth — "you."

She's holding her stare, and Jack's holding his. His pulse rate has risen. He and Elly have definitely come to something now.

"Do you want things to be as they were?" he asks.

She shakes her head slightly and waits for him to go on.

"Elly, I need you to tell me what you have in mind."

Elly gives him another rueful smile. "Tell me what you think I have in mind, Jack." Then she laughs. "No, I guess that isn't fair." She settles herself, looks at him, then down at her lap. She's blushing — which makes Jack feel such affection for her that he's tempted to say, *No, it's all right, Elly; you don't have to talk. I'm sorry I asked you.* He has to force himself to say nothing.

She clears her throat. "In Rome, something happened to me, Jack. I got away from myself. I didn't know anybody. Unless I hung out at the academy, I didn't hear much English. Nobody knew me or cared about me. I wasn't in a mood to make friends. I wanted to do my work — I was writing a long piece about these primitive artists — and to stay to myself. So I did. Each day was like floating farther off into space, drifting away from the world I was familiar with. And I understood that I've always been surrounded by people I knew — people who've given me my sense of who I am. The more time I spent alone, the less certain I was about who I was. It was like being without mirrors. After I got used to it, it wasn't a bad experience. I could be anybody. Or I could be one person one day and another the next — whoever I felt like being each morning when I woke up.

"One night I went to the opera at the Baths of Caracalla. It was summer, tickets were hard to get — the academy had one to give away, and I'd claimed it. Pavarotti was in town, and the performance had been sold out for months. Even though I'd become used to crowds in Rome, that mass of people was shocking to me. But these were wealthy and stylish people, jammed together in that outdoor theater like cattle in a stockyard. I found myself sitting beside a Japanese man, who asked for my help with something he couldn't understand in the program. As I was struggling to understand him — and just about to ask if he spoke English — it came to me that he thought I was Italian. No Italian would ever make such a mistake, but this man knew so little of the language and the culture that unless I corrected him, he would go on thinking of me as Italian. At first it was too much trouble to tell him I wasn't what he thought I was. But as he kept trying to communicate with me — in his comical version of Italian — I began to like being this other person. I could sort of see her, too, an upper-class, worldly Italian divorcée. And I began to find the man attractive. That was something that hadn't happened to me in a while — being drawn to a man. The encounter was almost like a costume ball or a carnival.

"I was attracted to the man mostly because I was another person in his eyes. But he did have a stocky ruggedness that I liked, and a beautifully tailored suit. And even if he'd figured out that I was an American academic, there'd still have been a huge cultural distance between us. As it was, with the two of us trying to use Italian, we were basically alien to each other, and I found that exciting. We had to communicate with our hands, our faces, our bodies, even our tone of voice. I was right in the mood to go with it. Parts of me came alive that I hadn't known existed.

"I won't bore you with all the details, Jack, but the evening ended exactly where you'd have expected it to, in a bed at the most expensive hotel in Rome. What may surprise you is that it was my one sexual adventure in the entire year I spent in Europe. The sex was fine, or, anyway, okay. And it was exhausting enough to give me a good night's sleep. When I woke up, of course, my partner was gone, as you might also have expected. I didn't mind. I hadn't wanted to keep play-acting in daylight.

"What I minded — it startled me — was the stack of currency neatly placed on top of my slip beside the bed. After I counted it, I decided that it was more money than the highest-priced call girl in Rome would have made for a week's worth of sex. I should have been flattered by the amount, but just its being there was troublesome.

"Of course I laughed. My partner had seen a person entirely different from the one I'd pretended to be, so I told myself that if I'd been playing the part of an expensive call girl — which I certainly wasn't above doing — I ought to be delighted with my success.

"All day I was amused. I put on the clothes I'd worn to the opera — I had no choice, of course — and their scent kept reminding me of the evening and the man. I kept those clothes on all through the morning and the afternoon. I went shopping and spent the money on new clothes, much more expensive ones than I'd have bought with money I'd earned 'legitimately.' In fact, Jack, the yellow dress and black scarf I wore to your office this morning were bought with my evening's wages from Mr. Noriguchi. I enjoyed the shopping — it was one more role to play, the American tourist with too much money to spend. But even with that fun, I felt more and more disturbed as the day went on. *I'm wasting my life* was the sentence that kept flashing in my mind, and I whispered the words to myself as I walked through the city. If there's such a thing as an involuntary mantra, that's exactly what I had for the days that followed: *I'm wasting my life. I'm wasting my life. I'm wasting my life.*"

Elly is quiet, but she's not looking directly at Jack, so he's comfortable enough to wait her out. Finally she shakes her head and goes on.

"Maybe everybody comes to a point like that, a time when you see everything in a clear light. What I saw was how I've made nearly every major decision of my adult life in a state of romantic delusion. I get into a mindset appropriate for a thirteen-year-old. Not only that, but the people I've given my best self to — namely, my former husbands — were equally deluded."

Elly's lips twitch into an expression somewhere between a smile and a grimace, but it vanishes almost instantly. Then her eyes focus on Jack, with such intensity that he can't meet them.

"The one person who ever saw me for who I actually am is you, Jack," she says.

Jack considers her point, then nods.

"And I'm pretty sure I saw you for what you are, too." She pauses to let that sink in.

"We're neither one of us very pretty," she murmurs. "By most people's standards."

Jack again considers her point before he nods in agreement. He waits. But he sees she's not going to continue, so he says, "I do see what you mean, Elly."

The look Elly gives him is one that Jack knows would be considered cold or harsh by anyone else. He takes it as a sign that Elly has him pegged right, that she has the two of them "accurately evaluated," to use a phrase from one of his marketing reports. So he sees — and admits to himself — that his life is about to change.

"What about Suzanne?" he asks.

Elly turns to the window, which looks out over the lake and the mountains and the blue-going-to-pewter sky in the far distance. Her face takes on a peaceful expression.

"Fuck Suzanne," she murmurs.

The most astounding discovery of La Tour's long life is Vivienne's uncovered back. She has what he calls the "wolf shoulder." He's seen it twice now, and was shocked even the second time. When he studies it in his mind, he's horrified, yet the girl's shoulder is all he thinks about these days.

Vivienne has been utterly cooperative about posing, so much so that La Tour wonders whether she has ever considered refusing to do what he asks. He should be happier about her willingness to please him. The old painter knows that he could instruct her to strip away every piece of clothing, and strike one immodest pose after another, and she would obey him. Were he so inclined, he could direct her to commit lewd acts, and she would do as he asked, though she is so innocent, he knows he would have to give her explicit instructions about the acts — a thought that makes him shudder. No model of his acquaintance, not even the remarkable Francine of his Magdalen period of twenty years ago, has approached Vivienne's tractability. He had become accustomed to some resistance — real or pretended or flirtatious — in the women who posed for him. Vivienne, however, seems markedly unusual in showing no reluctance to do as he asks.

He suspects she's this way only with him, as if she believes him to be almost as holy as the Pope. Which makes La Tour wonder whether he may be the unnatural one.

Perhaps he is, La Tour thinks, because he recognizes Vivienne's wolf shoulder as a natural phenomenon — strange but natural nonetheless. What is unnatural is how he is drawn to it, obsessed with it, his mind consumed with its image.

When he began to pose her, he had explained that he would draw some studies before he began the major composition. So he had directed her to lift her skirt to expose one thigh and then two. This, he realized, was what he had come to as an old man, teasing himself, trying to keep alive the only part of himself that he cared about. He had had her open her dress and expose her bosom down nearly to her nipples. Then, with his sketching materials, he had walked near the girl, intending merely to pretend to sketch but, in spite of himself (the pain in his arm discouraged him severely, and his heart thumped like a schoolboy's), scratching on the paper an image of Vivienne's chest.

He asked her to wear, the following day, a dress with buttons down the back so that she could open it and let him sketch her back. She had done so. And when the time came for the posing, she told him he would have to undo the two buttons between her shoulder blades, which she couldn't reach. He had done so. When the dress was open across her back — she had no garment beneath it — there, half a meter from his eyes, was a triangular pattern of dark hair that swept like a brush stroke across her right shoulder blade over to her spine and halfway down toward the small of her back. The pattern disappeared before it reached the top of her shoulder or her underarm. But directly behind her, where it would be hardest to touch, the hair was short, nearly as thick as a dog's. It had a tidiness in its downward pointing, each strand at the same angle, as if someone had combed the hair to lie that way.

The sight of it, when he pushed aside her dress, stopped La Tour from moving. He held his breath, as if he were underwater, and stood with his fingers still holding the cheap fabric of her dress. Vaguely he wondered whether he dared touch the silky pelt, which lay only centimeters from his hand. Then he noticed Vivienne turning slightly.

"Sir?" she said quietly.

She didn't know. She couldn't see it herself. And no one had told her! La Tour's fingers twitched when that realization came to him. *How did they keep her from knowing?* This feature of her own body was something of which the girl was completely unaware. Her parents must have gone to immense trouble to preserve Vivienne's ignorance of what was on her back.

That was when La Tour tried to calculate his allotted time. If he's lucky, he may have another four or five years of mobility and alertness; he wants to spend as many hours as possible in Vivienne's presence. What most concerns him is that the girl will notice the change in him and come to disrespect him. He can hardly bring himself to give her any orders or directions. When she comes to his studio in the mornings now, he has a desire to kneel before her.

Suzanne is shocked, when she glances at her watch, to see that her office hours are almost over. So much time has passed! "I'm sinking deeper into this," she whispers to herself with a shudder. She wonders whether eventually she'll lose control, whether reverie will take over her every waking moment.

Last year a colleague asked why she had stopped leaving her door open during office hours. Suzanne laughed politely and said she hadn't really thought about it; perhaps she was too old to care whether her students came to consult her. In fact, she has never enjoyed discussions with students in her office, even those she likes and admires. One-to-one meetings with them make her uneasy, make her feel as if she's expected to give the visitor some knowledge she doesn't possess.

Nevertheless, she knows her students are entitled to her time, so she dutifully goes to her office and waits. Apparently some part of her consciousness has determined that a closed office door will discourage all but the most determined. It may be the same part of her mind that constructs the imaginative excursions in which, more and more, she finds herself lost. With the door closed, office hours have become a time when she feels obliged to do nothing but sit and wait. If no visitors appear, then her mind goes where it wishes. Today, she's pursuing the invention that began to charm her when she planned to write the essay on Georges de La Tour. She admits to herself that all through the morning class, she was looking forward to returning to La Tour and Vivienne. She's surprised and pleased that the old man has become so taken with the girl.

"I'm reverting to childhood," she tells herself, gathering up her papers to go to her next class, a senior seminar. She remembers that, when she was little, one of her greatest pleasures was making up dreams as she fell asleep. She adored the moment when her mother tucked the bedcovers around her, kissed her good night, turned out the light, and tiptoed from her room, easing the door shut. She wonders whether it was because her parents didn't read to her that she made up her own stories in the dark. "Which is exactly what I'm doing with this old bastard La Tour," she says to herself, smiling grimly as she steps into the hallway, filled with students and colleagues moving between classes. "Terrible thing, when you're almost forty and behave as you did at age six."

*

When Jack leaves Elly's hotel room, around one in the afternoon, he feels that in this single morning he's lived several lifetimes. After breakfast, he and Elly took their time making love. Elly, determined to delight him, had whispered to him, had moved him beyond what he thought were the limits of his sexual capacity. Now he feels as if he's floating on the street. Could it have been too much for him, having all that sex in so short a time? Though he wants to stride purposefully toward his office, his legs feel rubbery, and everything looks either too vague or too intensely clear. Faces lurch into his vision out of nowhere, and he's startled by them. They look distorted, alien.

After Jack and Elly finally got around to it, they drew up their plans quickly. Tonight he's to tell Suzanne he's moving out. He'll try to work out some of the details with her. If she's too upset, then he'll say they can discuss the details later. But no matter what, he'll be moving to the Radisson tomorrow. When he gets back to the office this afternoon, he'll call the clients whose appointments he missed this morning, and then ask his secretary to cancel his appointments for tomorrow. Things will be chaotic around his office for a while.

Jack knows that splitting up with Suzanne will be ugly. When he asked Elly whether it might be better to proceed slowly and make less of a spectacle of themselves, Elly looked straight at him and said, in her softest, most patient tone of voice, "Darling, it wants to be ugly. It wants to be just ugly enough to last." Jack didn't reply. He knew she was right.

Each morning when Vivienne arrives at the studio, La Tour's dogs make a terrific commotion. The girl takes their barking as a greeting. When Vivienne first began coming, La Tour taught her all the dogs' names, so now when she walks into his courtyard, she speaks affectionately to each one. They grovel at her feet, rolling over and displaying their bellies, tucking down their tails, and slavishly showing her their teeth. The old painter knows the villagers hate his dogs, and he had first thought that introducing them to the shoemaker's daughter was a way to twit the townspeople. Although he no longer thinks of Vivienne as one of those wretched Lunévillians, her control over his dogs makes him uneasy. He considers them his little army.

Today he has set up two chairs by the window. It's a bright day; the light will be delicious. She's become accustomed to his gazing at her for long periods of time and only occasionally moving his pencil across the tablet in his lap. What she seems to like best is his quiet questioning. He may say, "Vivienne, I would like you to describe the meal you would most enjoy if you could have anything you wanted."

She will pause and then, in a dreamy voice, describe a certain way the meat must be cooked, list the seasonings that should be on the vegetables, the various breads that should be served with her meal, and — oh, pleasure of pleasures! — the tarts and puddings for her dessert and the sauces that go with them and nuts and cheeses . . .

La Tour has discovered that Vivienne enjoys answering his food question again and again. Each time, she concocts a different meal. It has become evident to him that when she leaves the studio, she ponders the question, improves her answers, and waits for him to ask it again. Vivienne must savor the chance to talk — perhaps not to him; perhaps it wouldn't matter who listened to her lilting voice shaping her fanciful sentences. But he's certain he is the only one who has asked such questions of her or been interested in what she may have to say about such matters as what she likes to eat, where she would like to travel, and what clothes she dreams of wearing.

"Vivienne, I want you to describe a perfect day, a whole day in which each thing that happens is just to your liking."

The girl's face brightens while she considers the request. Then, as she begins to speak, La Tour rises from his chair, goes to her, gently opens two buttons of her blouse — she hardly pays attention to him — loosens it around her shoulders, and turns her slightly so that he can study the effect of sunlight on her wolf's shoulder yet still see her profile as she talks.

"Sir, it would begin with no one waking me in the morning and with such quiet in the house that I could sleep as long as I wished. After I woke but was still lying in my bed, gazing at the ceiling, I would call out to Maman, and she would bring me coffee with milk that came from our neighbor's cow no more than an hour before. Maman would sit beside me and talk while I drank my coffee, and she would tell me . . ."

At such moments, La Tour is on the verge of complete happiness. At first he doesn't know how to accept it. But when it does come to him, it frightens him. "I can't," he says to himself. "I'm too old," he whispers loudly enough to make Vivienne pause.

"Sir?" she says softly.

La Tour stirs in his chair and tries to calm himself, not reveal how disturbed he is. "Nothing. Nothing, my dear. Please go on. You were speaking of the picnic that would take place early in the afternoon?"

Sam dances in circles in front of Suzanne, wriggling and whimpering and bumping her legs with his rump, while she pats his back and head, crooning to him, "Oh, you sweet darling; you are the best dog of all time; you are the dog my dreams." She sets down her purse and briefcase and kneels on the floor to be at eye-level with him, though of course Sam doesn't want to sit still or look her in the eye. Then she lets him out into the back yard and watches with amusement while he pees at length, gazing at her over his shoulder. "Good boy!" she calls.

Suzanne loves the still house. She knows that one reason she had such difficulty adjusting to Sam was that the puppy dispossessed her of her solitude. She would never again have the house to herself. Now she knows that it's okay; no, it's better. When she comes home, Sam makes a big fuss over her, so she doesn't encounter the loneliness that sometimes hit her when she entered the empty house. And after a few minutes, he settles down, stays near her, but becomes invisible, requiring no attention yet ready to provide her with distraction if she wants it.

"I do have the perfect situation, don't I?" she tells Sam while filling his water dish. And as she looks down at the dog's soulful face, she thinks of Jack. Standing at the sink, Suzanne experiences a piercing moment, an absurdly vivid remembrance of an afternoon early in their marriage.

Jack was teaching her to play tennis; she hated him for cheerfully ignoring her mistakes. She wanted him to yell at her, to tell her that she stank beyond belief — because she knew that's what she deserved. Was he a fool? Couldn't he acknowledge what an oaf she was with a tennis racquet? If she hit the ball hard, it sailed away; if she hit it carefully, it poofed into the net. Never did the ball go where she wanted it to go. And all Jack did was say, gently, "Move your feet, turn your body, get your racquet ready, keep your eye on the ball, . . ." Across the net from her, he had a basket of balls, each of which he stroked softly to her, one after another, precisely to where it would be easy for her to reach and stroke it back to him. Yet all she could do was flail wildly, and the closest Jack came to criticizing her was to chuckle when she socked one poor ball far over the backstop into the trees behind him.

"WOULD YOU PLEASE —" Suzanne never got to finish that sentence, because when she turned sharply — to present her back to him at the same time as she screamed up to the sky to let him know in no uncertain terms how fed up she was with his hypocrisy in these stupid circumstances — she stepped hard on a tennis ball, twisted her ankle, and fell to the hard surface in such a spasm of pain that she blacked out.

When, a moment later, she was conscious, she felt the pain all over her body, down to her fingertips and out to the ends of her hair. It radiated up from the ankle, which someone must have chopped with an ax. She thought she was going to vomit.

Jack picked her up, carried her to the car, and drove her straight to the emergency room. He left their racquets and the basket of tennis balls at the court, and the racquets were stolen, though Jack told her the balls were lying all over the place when he went back later that afternoon. He was much amused, though she wasn't. She saw it as further evidence of her hopeless incompetence at the sport that was integral to her young husband's life and personality. The racquets were expensive, and it was her fault that they'd been stolen. Jack was no more upset about their loss than he was over the ball she'd hit into the trees beyond the backstop.

The tenderness Jack showed her when he first ran to help her was like nothing she'd experienced before. When she saw his face, she knew he felt how much her ankle hurt her; she knew he hated her pain. Later, while they waited in the emergency room for the nurse to bring her a pair of crutches, he held her hand and told her, "I'm so sorry, my darling." It may not have been an original thing to say, but she recognized it as the truth. Jack truly was deeply sorry that she was in pain. During all their courtship and their months of marriage before that afternoon, she hadn't been aware of his powerful caring. She had never been the object of such care from another human being.

"That was quite something," Suzanne tells the dog as she sets the water dish in front of him. She's enough shaken by the memory to go to the living room and sit still for a while.

*

[*57*]

Jack's walking home. He fled the office. His secretary, Eva, asked where he'd been all morning, and though he prides himself on being an accomplished liar, he could think of nothing credible to tell her. He nearly blurted out, *I was naked in a hotel room with my old lover.* He may as well have done so, because when he ignored her question, he could see her face telling him, *You were with a woman, weren't you?* She raised her good Catholic eyebrows. Though Eva has never said so directly, she's made it clear to Jack that she considers his private life a mess. As far as he can tell, she disapproves of both his marriage and his infidelity. Were she not a superior worker, he could have got rid of her long ago. As her form of criticism, Eva managed to put through to him one hostile phone call after another, mostly from the clients who'd been scheduled to see him that morning, while she kept pressing him to keep his afternoon appointments. It was when she was buzzing him again to pick up the phone that Jack plucked his jacket off the coat tree by the door and walked out. "Gettin' outa this hell hole," he murmured as he walked past her desk.

When he's left the building and turned the corner up by the Y, he remembers that he's supposed to be on the tennis court right this minute. Pat Clayton isn't the kind of guy you stand up for a tennis match — unless you want to hear about it under the most embarrassing circumstances for the next six months. Pat's a lawyer with a loud mouth and a get-even mentality. Well, there's nothing Jack can do about it now, but he feels his face grow red as he pictures Pat in his tennis whites, pacing and muttering, out on Court Number 2 at the club. They always play on the second most visible court, so his absence is humiliating Pat in front of their whole crowd of tennis acquaintances.

Jack comes to a halt on the sidewalk in front of Dolan House on South Union Street. *What the hell am I up to?* he asks himself. Over the years, he has put together a life that is intricate but of exemplary orderliness. Suddenly it's a shambles. In a single day, he's alienated half a dozen business associates, plunged his office into chaos, and sabotaged his long-time tennis pal. And this is even before he sits down to inform Suzanne, his wife of a dozen years, that he's moving out of their house and leaving their marriage. *Do I love Elly Jacobs enough to do this?* He can't take another step toward home until he's answered the question.

Yes! No! I don't know! Each answer seems right. Standing in the late afternoon sunlight of a spring day in Burlington, Vermont, Jack Nelson is paralyzed.

". . . and no matter how much I begged, Maman never let me go to the river to bathe with everyone else. Instead, she would take me with her on days when it was so chilly that she knew no one in the village would be there. 'Your rare beauty,' she would say, 'may make some terrible person wish to hurt you if he sees you bathing. You must promise me you will never expose yourself to anyone, not even to your cousins.'

"You see, sir, Maman and Papa wanted to have many children, and before me there were some babies who couldn't wait long enough to be born, and there was one who waited and was born but died the next day. So when I came to them and stayed alive, I made them very happy. Then after me there were no more babies. I think I must be the only girl in Lunéville who has no brothers or sisters. Maman and Papa always want me to stay at home. When I was little, they didn't allow me to play with my cousins, though when I cried, they sometimes let me — if one of my aunts promised to keep an eye on me. My cousins treated me as if I were made of glass and would break if they so much as touched me.

"The afternoon you came to see my Papa? After you went away, after they stood watching you walk back through the village with all your dogs around you, there was such a discussion between my parents that it frightened me. They went up to their bedroom to talk, and they made me stay downstairs in the shop, but after a while I could hear Maman weeping and Papa raising his voice to her. So I slipped over to the bottom of the stairs, where I could hear them better and still see anyone who came into the shop.

"Maman was so upset, she was nearly screaming. 'She's my only baby! You know what he wants to do to her! You know!' And Papa was saying, 'He's not going to hurt her. Don't you know, they say he's a saint? He has to be, or he could not make God come into those pictures he paints. They say the Pope sent a messenger to ask him to paint a picture. And anyway, Monsieur La Tour is an old man and can't do anything to her.' Sir, I hope you don't mind my telling you these things.

"When they finally came down to the shop to talk to me, my Papa explained that I was to come here each morning, as you had asked, to let you paint me, and that I was to do just what you told me to do and remember my best manners when I am here, because you are like the bishop who came here last year. Then my Maman cried and said it was because I am not like other girls that you had come to our shop to ask my father's permission to put me in your pictures. And Papa said that if you asked to see me without my clothes, I should let you do so, even though I might not want to and even though they had told me never to let anyone see me. Papa said that when you asked me, I should pretend to be someone else, someone in a picture, because that is what I will be. While Papa was explaining these things to me, Maman turned away and put her face in her hands.

"But you see, sir, it has not been the way I thought it would be. I was afraid at first. And I know Maman and even Papa were afraid, too. Every afternoon when I came home, they greeted me with questions and with worried faces. After they saw I was all right, they became cheerful, but they still had questions; they wanted to know everything you had said and everything you had asked me to do. They made me tired, the way they hovered around me. At first I told them — not everything, but some things that would interest them. I told them about your dogs, because I knew they didn't want to hear about them and if I talked too long about the dogs, they would leave me alone.

"I have never told them that you ask me questions and listen to me when I talk — and how it pleases me to tell you these things. It's so strange; I don't even know how to explain it to myself, let alone to Maman and Papa. When I start to answer one of your questions, I don't know what I'm going to say. Do you remember the first one you asked me, sir? You wanted to know about my room at home, how it looked, where the bed was, where the window was, how the light came through it, where I put everything, and whether there was a place to hang my dresses. It was so easy to tell you! That old quilt my aunt made — I told you about it, how its faded colors are so pretty when the sun comes in my window, how I chewed on it when I was a little girl, how I still like to put it against my cheek in the morning when I wake up. And I told you about the little shirts Maman made for me that I always wore, even in the summer, and how she told me she made them because she loved me so much.

"How could I tell anyone else about those silly little private matters? Who would ever ask me about them? Or who would listen if I started to talk about them? And, sir, I must tell you, I wouldn't even have known I had so many belongings — all the things you've asked me about — if you hadn't asked me. I'll tell you what it was like, sir! Until you began to ask me about

[*61*]

my life, I never saw it, because to me it was invisible. I could have lived to be an old lady without a glimpse of what my life was like.

"So I think they were right, Maman and Papa, when they told me you were like the bishop. Except that I was afraid of the bishop, and though I was afraid of you, too, at first, now I am not afraid at all! Whatever the opposite of afraid is, that's what I am now. Every day I want to come here. I'm ready for you to ask me anything. I know sometimes you don't think about it; you ask me whatever comes into your mind. At home, I often wonder about what I want you to ask me, and sometimes it happens just that way — you ask what I'd hoped you would. You'll never guess what I hope you'll ask me now. Is this the way you want me to turn my shoulder, sir? I'm sorry; I know I sometimes get careless about how I stand. I'm not tired. I could stand like this all day. But it is so much easier when you give me a question. Do you have another one for me today? Does this look all right now, sir?"

La Tour is in such pain that he knows he cannot stand at his easel another five minutes. He hasn't thought of another question for the girl today. When they began this morning, he had no idea that they would work so long. Now, both his shoulders feel as if the joints have become lumps of burning charcoal. His right hip smolders, too. Still, he has managed to put a little paint on the canvas. Whenever he glances at it, the picture draws him in. He's almost able to forget his pain when he sees how Vivienne is coming to life on the surface before him; how, in spite of everything wrong with him, he is making the girl live in his picture.

La Tour would shrug if he weren't in such pain. Painting has never before felt this way to him. *This* picture is making him do what *it* wants; this picture is demanding everything he has ever learned. The old painter knows that all he should do is stand before it, his palette and his brush ready; what's in front of him will tell him what next to do. The work amazes him, because, although it is slow and he accomplishes little each day, it makes no difference to the picture. It's like a dream growing ever more vivid. All it wants is patience. All it wants — La Tour knows this — is for him to live long enough to finish it. He knows well that this will be his last piece. And he finds the thought a great relief. "I am the one who stands here," he whispers to himself. "I am the one with eyes and hands." He raises his brush, touches the canvas once here, once there, waits, studies it, touches the palette, raises the brush again.

Vivienne holds the yellow cloth to her front. She stands sideways, her head turned toward him as if she has just realized he sees her. Her expression is one of extreme alertness and curiosity. In this moment, modesty has caused her to raise the drapery, but she has no fear. The portrait is of her full length, the whole of her back, her skin taking the light from the unseen window — her skin the light itself. As La Tour has come to understand it, the picture's true purpose is to demonstrate light becoming flesh. Except for the young woman herself and the bright yellow cloth, everything is brown or midnight black. There are no background details; she is surrounded by darkness. La Tour hasn't yet set the wolf's hair on Vivienne's shoulder, because each day when they finish, Vivienne comes around to the front of his easel and, while she dresses, looks at the picture. She's quiet; she says nothing. La Tour knows the wolf's shoulder is to come. He's going to do it. Eventually. And he knows that when he has set down that extraordinary sunlit glistening of the dark thatch on Vivienne's shoulder, the picture will be finished. *He* will be finished.

"Tell me —" He must clear his throat, because the pain is constricting his voice. "Tell me, Vivienne, about going to Mass with your Maman and Papa. I know you do. Tell me how you get up on Sunday morning, and how the three of you get dressed and what you say to one another. Do you have something to drink before you leave the house? Does your Maman fix the coffee as usual? Tell me every bit."

"Oh, sir," Vivienne begins, and the happiness of her voice takes away all La Tour's pain.

Jack remembers Elly's greeting to him one afternoon several years ago: "Jack, you cotton-mouthed numbskull! Do you even think about what you're saying? Do I look like somebody who wants to make small talk with you?"

It's a disturbing recollection. What came next was that Elly whacked him near the shoulder with her palm. Because of where her hand hit — on the fleshy part of his upper arm — it stung more than it hurt. She'd swung plenty hard enough to hurt him if she'd hit almost anywhere else. Jack was shocked. All he'd done was step into her apartment and say, "How's your day going, sweetheart?"

"My day, for your information, has been a total catastrophe. My day has been the day of an idiot, the day of a moron, the day of a nincompoop. My day has been a stinker and a screamer and a bloody blue-plate pisser. But I was coping with it pretty damn well until you waltzed in here with no eyes and half your brain and your stupid mouth making noises like grocery store music!"

Then she whacked him on the other arm. If she'd been a man, Jack would have either hit her or walked away. As it was, he stood in the middle of her living room, with his arms crossed, rubbing both shoulders while he tried to figure out what the hell was going on. Now he wondered why he hadn't noticed right off that Elly was wilder than he'd ever seen her. Her hair was up in a top-knot, strands sticking out every which way. Her eyes were red, and her face was raw, as if she'd been rubbing it. As far as Jack could tell, all she had on was a ripped T-shirt, which he would later call her Hell Shirt, a thing she never washed but kept on the floor of her closet to be dug out and put on when she was feeling wretched. The old shirt had a nasty smell. Elly, standing opposite him, tried to tug it farther down over her thighs and glared at him as if he'd called her an ugly name.

"WILL YOU PLEASE SAY SOMETHING THAT MATTERS TO SOMEBODY SOMEWHERE ON THE FACE OF THE PLANET?" she shrieked.

Elly has gone crazy, Jack thought. Only a little more than a week before, they'd become lovers. Now Jack could see he'd got himself involved with somebody loony enough to scare him.

"I'm sorry, Elly —"

"I DON'T NEED YOUR —" Elly's voice reached a crescendo of shrillness and broke off. Her mouth twisted open. Tears began to spill out of her terrible eyes.

He stepped forward, put his arms around her, pulled her to his chest. At first, she was stiff as a mannequin, but then her body softened, as if she'd let the life flow back into it. Jack didn't know how he'd understood to go to her, hold her like that. He did it, and it was the right thing. It was the only act that could have helped Elly.

"My dad's sick," Elly sobbed into his chest. "My dad's real sick."

Jack said nothing. He led her to the sofa, sat down with her, held her, and let her talk, let her tell him about her father — who was in a hospital in Texas with what the doctors thought was cancer. Elly didn't want to talk about the hospital — she was flying down there that evening. "I'll have enough of that when I get there," she said. She wanted to tell him sentimental stuff — what her daddy had done for her when she was little, like walking her to kindergarten every day and buying her the cookies she liked and playing Chutes and Ladders with her and letting her cheat. This weepy sentimental Elly was someone he hadn't seen or imagined — her "soft side," as he later came to think of it. The crazy tantrum with which she'd greeted him somehow caused him to appreciate her. He sat quietly and held her and rubbed her back. And a little later, he teased her about the smell of her Hell Shirt.

Elly sniffled, sat up, looked at him, and grinned. "Well, you can take it off," she said.

"What?"

She raised her arms over her head. "Take it off."

Walking up Pearl Street this late afternoon, Jack, still in the spell of remembering how charmed he was that day by Elly, is only vaguely aware of where he is now. He has to remind himself that he's going home to change his life. He's going home to tell Suzanne he's leaving. And when he turns the corner, trying to focus his mind, it's as if Suzanne is somebody he read about weeks or months ago.

Suzanne wonders whether she should be more worried about herself. She's in her living room with a magazine open on her lap, but some minutes ago she'd stopped reading. The old memory of Jack and her sprained ankle has made her start taking stock of her life. She has her health and her looks. She and Jack have more than enough money. She has this well-furnished house and this faithful dog curled beside her chair in this pleasant room. The book that she worked on for so long, *European Background: Peripheral Symbolism in Caravaggio, Terbrugghen, and La Tour,* will finally be published in the fall, by Cornell University Press. By the time she's thirty-eight, she'll be promoted to full professor, which means that even if she isn't a natural-born teacher, the University of Vermont still thinks she's hot stuff. Suzanne knows she's writing better than ever before, and she knows it's because her imagination is more inclined to take off on forays into the world of the pictures she's writing about. However coincidental that may be, she's found that her daydreams help her create the narrative-based criticism that no one else is writing. She's considered the most daring of the New Scholars of sixteenth- and seventeenth-century painting.

And of course she has Jack. Suzanne figures that Jack is on his way home this very minute to cook dinner for her. "That's how I have him," she tells herself with a wry grin. "He lives in the same house I do; he cooks me dinner. He brings me coffee and the newspaper in the morning. Though we used to have to talk to each other, now he only makes insipid remarks. But he does stay out of my way — most of the time."

She sits with that thought for a moment, meaning to give herself a twinge by measuring how distant she is from him after their having been close when they were first married.

"So Jack is the one thing about my life that I've screwed up," she tells herself and immediately smiles again, acknowledging that if she and Jack were still close, she wouldn't be spending so much time in her own head. She wouldn't be writing well, and she wouldn't be expecting her promotion.

"It's Jack or La Tour, I suppose," she says to the empty room. "And right now I'm more married to La Tour than I am to Jack." As she says it, she sees the old painter closing his eyes and arrogantly nodding, as if to say of course that's the way it is. Any sensible person would choose him over a superficial oaf like her husband.

Sam lifts his head and gives her a look.

"You're right, puppy. It's sick," Suzanne admits quietly.

La Tour has no idea how long he's been working; the girl stopped talking some time ago, after he failed to think of another question. She stands frozen in her pose, her face as it is supposed to be, but for the first time in their days of working together, she's gazing straight through him. Whatever it is she sees, it isn't he. La Tour is jolted at the thought of himself as merely an object in her line of vision. The monstrous pain in his back and hips and shoulders has shaken him back to conscious thought; he feels as if he's been trampled by a horse. A moan rises in him, but before he can utter it, he realizes that he must set Vivienne's wolf shoulder on the canvas — now. He must do it this instant!

He watches the tip of his smallest brush stroking darkness onto the bright swatch of light in the middle of the canvas. It touches again and again.

The brush slips from his fingers. This amuses La Tour. There is no need to pick it up. He lets the palette fall on the other side. That, too, is funny. He collapses into his chair. Weeks ago he'd moved the chair next to the easel so that, at the end of each working day, he could sit down and watch Vivienne as she picked up her clothes and came over to dress while evaluating the painting's progress. Now, in spite of his urge to groan or shriek or laugh, the old painter remains quiet.

Alarmed by the dropped brush and palette, the girl looks at him warily. He nods encouragingly. *Don't be alarmed,* he means to say, though he can't say the words aloud. She lets down her arms, which must be exhausted from holding the yellow drapery to her chest. It flickers across his mind that he must appear to her as a figure in a dream. She's trying to recognize him. He tries to smile.

Jack quietly enters his house the back way. He's all too aware of the door's squeak on its hinges, the change in light, the lingering scent that is the history of hundreds of meals he and Suzanne have eaten in this house. He's been trying to focus his thoughts on his wife, on how she'll look when he tells her what he must tell her, on what she'll say — he can imagine whole paragraphs of terrible things Suzanne may say about Elly and him. What's odd is that Jack's brain refuses to bring him the sight of her. As he walked up the hill to the corner and then down his street, he saw every brick, clapboard, every blade of grass, but, try as he did, he wasn't able to bring to mind the face of his wife.

He steps into the living room; Suzanne is sitting in the wing chair that faces him. Sam is lying on the floor beside her, his head lifted toward Jack and his ears perked up and his tail wagging. Jack knows the dog is glad to see him, but he can't tell about Suzanne. Though she's looking straight at him, Jack wonders whether she actually sees him or is caught up in her thoughts with her eyes frozen in his direction. She's wearing the white blouse and dark blazer and skirt from her teaching day. She's sitting up straight, her knees together and her hands folded in her lap, as if she's been waiting for him — or somebody. Suzanne is the only person he knows who can relax in a formal pose. But her face doesn't tell Jack anything. It's composed.

"Do you remember what you said this morning when I brought your coffee and newspaper?" Jack asks. His voice is calm, but he has no idea why this question occurred to him.

Suzanne's eyes change focus. He understands that she's examining his face now, trying to fathom what he's up to. He also knows that he was right in suspecting that even when he stepped into this room, he wasn't in her thoughts. She shakes her head.

"I can't either," Jack says. "All the way home, I've been trying to remember what you said to me this morning, and you know what I think?"

Again Suzanne shakes her head.

"I don't think you said anything at all. I don't think you said 'Good morning' or 'Thanks for the paper' or 'What's the weather like' or anything."

When he stops, the silence lies between them.

"I'm sorry, Jack," she finally murmurs.

Her voice startles him; its softness hurts him a little. It has indeed been a long time since he's heard her speak to him. He has an impulse to lift his hand and wave away the conversation, to say, *No big deal. I know it takes you a while to wake up.* He is about to say just that when he has an image of Elly, Elly in her yellow dress, standing at his office door, Elly blushing and drinking him in with her eyes, as if she can't get enough of him.

"Elly's back," Jack blurts. He feels his heartbeat speed up.

Jack doesn't know what his face is telling her — maybe everything. But her face tells him nothing.

"I see," she says. Then, carefully, lifting one eyebrow in that way of hers, she says, "I do see, don't I?"

Jack nods.

In the hanging silence, a peculiar coincidence occurs. Jack kneels to pat Sam's head at the same moment that Suzanne reaches down to touch the dog. Neither pulls back, so for about twenty seconds, the dog has Jack's hand on his head and Suzanne's on his shoulder. Sam thumps the floor with his tail. *Moment of paradise, huh, buddy?* Jack thinks, but the seriousness of the situation keeps him from saying it.

Suzanne lifts her hand in nearly the same gesture Jack had imagined doing a moment ago to wave away the conversation. "I think you ought to go to her," she says. She keeps looking at him; there is no blaze of anger, no tight smile of regret. Her face remains neutral.

"I was going to suggest that," Jack says. He waits a moment to see what else Suzanne may say, but she presses her lips together and turns her face toward the window. Jack can almost feel her thoughts moving away from him. *Come back,* he wants to call out, but he doesn't know what those words mean, and he certainly couldn't explain them to Suzanne, who would turn that polite face to him and ask, *What did you say, Jack?*

He goes upstairs to pack.

When Vivienne steps in front of the easel, La Tour takes a deep breath, which he is unable to release as she stands before the picture. Her mouth is slightly open, her eyes are turned upward. For a long moment, the only movement is that of her eyes as they move over the canvas. Then her right arm slowly begins to rise — almost involuntarily, as if, in a dream, she was reaching up to grasp something on a high shelf. Suddenly, her face contorts, and La Tour knows he could not have imagined that expression if he lived to be a hundred. Her right arm flies up and across her breasts — she stretches as far as she can — and her fingertip touches the place on her left shoulder he has just finished darkening. He exhales at the instant he sees her fingers touch the thatch of hair on her body. *So they kept her even from touching it,* he tells himself.

She whirls away from the picture to face him, still twisting her torso so that she touches the back of her shoulder. As if the old painter has thrown boiling water across her back, she screams at him. La Tour flinches, and she screams at him again and throws her body forward to lash at him with her wordless shrieking. He wishes he could walk away from her, but he isn't strong enough to stand up, nor can he make himself look away. The appalling distortion of her features tells La Tour something he's known but has never voiced to himself — that nothing expresses anguish like the human face. What a face can tell of joy or pleasure is slight compared with how sublimely it articulates pain.

Is this what I have lived all these years to witness? he asks himself. And without a moment's pause, the hateful answer comes. *Yes.*

Snatching up her clothes and clutching them to her chest, Vivienne gives him one last devastating look and runs from the studio. La Tour knows the girl well enough to understand that she'd rather dress out in his courtyard, where any beggar or carriage driver could see her, than spend another moment in his presence.

"Yes," he says aloud to the empty studio. "Yes," he says to the picture on the easel. "What did I expect you to do?" he asks it.

When Jack goes upstairs, Sam stays where he is, beside Suzanne's chair. Suzanne understands something that seems downright hilarious. If the dog had followed Jack up to their room, she would have stayed here in the living room, weeping. As it is, well, she wants to be cautious, but the idea that strikes her is that her life is about to undergo a major improvement. *I think I'm ready for this.* For an instant she considers running upstairs to share the revelation with Jack.

It's no wonder I've been lonely, Jack tells himself. He's facing his closet, deciding which shirts, jackets, slacks, and ties he should take now and which he can leave for later. But he's having trouble concentrating on the task. The puzzle is how easy Suzanne made that conversation. He's been a ghost in her life. *She'll hardly notice I'm gone.*

Well, that's all right. He directs his thoughts toward Elly. *That's just all right,* he tells himself firmly. He summons up Elly's face, the way she looked at him as he was leaving her hotel room. She was about to go to sleep, lying on her side, naked and snuggled in the bedcovers. The short lock of hair at her temple had fallen forward over her eye. That detail disturbs Jack, because he can't remember whether her eyes were open or closed when she said goodbye. Her voice was soft and sleepy, but he can't recall her mouth — was she smiling or looking sad? As he tries to recover the memory, her face dissolves in his mind's eye. What he does remember is her yellow dress, that gorgeously expensive yellow silk, flung carelessly across the chair beside the door. It was what Jack noticed as he left Elly's room.

Out in La Tour's courtyard, his dogs moil around Vivienne, seeking her attention while she sobs and tries to put on her clothes. "GET OUT OF MY — !" she shrieks at them. "YOU STINKING — !" Just as she's about to kick Caravaggio, she notices its bug-eyed devil's face and becomes amused. She's still crying; even so, she manages to laugh at herself for her absurd fury. "He's the one I should be trying to kick," she tells the dogs. "He's the animal. You dear souls are the very angels of Lunéville." She wipes her nose with the inside of her wrist. Now that she's buttoned her dress, she's glad that she had the presence of mind to snatch up her shoes before running out of the studio. She wouldn't want to walk barefoot through the village. As the fury rises in her again, she turns toward La Tour's studio and screams, "YOU OLD — !" But she can't think of a word bad enough for the painter — for what he did to her.

Vivienne reaches back to touch her shoulder. It interests her, how the place feels through the fabric of her dress. She stands still a moment, her fingers on the back of her shoulder, and tries to summon up its appearance in the painting. La Tour's dogs are quiet, waiting for her. They're accustomed to walking with Vivienne through the village to her father's shop, until one by one they turn and trot back toward the house where they will be fed.

Vivienne suddenly brings around her arm and points a finger at the dogs. They are the soldiers, and she is the general. "Stay here!" she shouts in a voice she knows they will obey. She jabs her finger at each one. "You stay!" she rasps. When she starts walking toward the center of the village, the dogs sit and watch her go.

As best she can while she walks, Vivienne arranges her hair and pats it into place. She looks down the front of her dress to see whether it looks right. She pulls at her skirt to make it hang evenly and fusses with her sleeves. As she walks, thoughts rise, one after another, and these carry her along. Before she's halfway home, she's humming the little song that she likes this week. It's so strange, the way her life is completely new this afternoon. Now that she knows about her shoulder — she reaches back to touch it again — she understands so many things! She smiles. How crazy her mother and father have been. Will she tell them that she knows? Or will she keep it from them? She can hardly wait to step into the shop and see their faces as they turn to her. She'll tell them — she knows that now. Already the words are coming into her mind. And, oh, how she will shout at them!

IV

SUZANNE WOULD HAVE BEEN fine, except that, without intention, the girls on her hall taught her about good clothes. Not according to the Galax and Stevens Creek standard, but that of Philadelphia and Atlanta and Dallas. Actually, it was the texture of fabric that changed Suzanne's taste — the succulent silk of Dulane Ponder's pale pink blouse, the luxurious herringbone tweed of Val Simms's tailored riding jacket, the cashmere of her roommate Sarah's charcoal gray cardigan. The cardigan in particular was so irresistible that one cold Saturday afternoon, when Sarah, gone for the weekend to Lexington, had left the sweater lying on the foot of her bed, Suzanne couldn't resist slipping it on. She didn't go to dinner that evening, because she knew she shouldn't be seen wearing Sarah's sweater, but she didn't want to take it off. As she studied late into the morning hours, the sweater kept her awake; she knew she'd have to take it off before she went to bed. It would be wrong to sleep in it.

Unlike the others on her hall, Suzanne had never borrowed clothes. Her sisters fiercely guarded the few desirable items they owned, and her mother hadn't allowed her daughters to "get into her things," as she put it. Suzanne hadn't had close friends in school to exchange clothes with, so she'd grown up with what she considered a pretty healthy view of personal property — you left other people's things alone. At Hollins, however, from her first hours on campus, she saw girls lending this and borrowing that. There was a giddy energy to the lending and borrowing, as if these young ladies from all around the country were suddenly grasping an opportunity.

Because her own clothes were undistinguished, Suzanne did not offer to lend them to anyone, nor did she ask to borrow anything. Nevertheless, she was brought into the exchanges. This was the fall of 1967, when "funky," as both a word and a concept, had found its way onto the Hollins campus. Upper-class white girls savored the word like verbal chocolate. Suzanne discovered that some of her clothes — the Peter Pan–collar no-iron blouses, for instance, which her mother had bought for her in yellow, pink, and blue at Leggett's — were desirable on the basis of their funkiness. So she entered the lending-borrowing fray with a grand giddiness all her own. Funky! My God, she thought, maybe her entire life, growing up in Stevens Creek, and riding a school bus twenty miles to and from high school in Galax, had been funky — and therefore remarkable in a way she'd never appreciated.

Suzanne's parents made a point of sending her only small amounts of money — a ten-dollar bill in a card from her mother, a twenty-five-dollar check from her father on her birthday. She understood perfectly well, and she didn't ask for more. Before she'd left home in August, she'd lorded it over them a bit — how she'd not be needing their help, because Hollins had granted her a full scholarship and a job in the library so that she could earn spending money. And now Suzanne had enough to buy snacks and essentials and go out occasionally with the girls on her hall. Also, she'd never been one to think much about money.

But in that winter of 1968, there were certain items of clothing that she did desire — a plaid skirt at Smyth's, a pair of tassel loafers at Davidson's, and, at the little boutique called Perfection, a set of black lacy underwear that made her blush when she thought of it. Over the months at college, when she accompanied her new friends on shopping expeditions into downtown Roanoke, she took note of these things, and later, felt that her wish for them was probably a diminishment of her innocent pre-Hollins self. Before, she wouldn't have known to want these things. But she figured that it was all right, that maybe it was a humbling force in her life, because the possibility of her owning those clothes was out of the question. She'd never have enough money to buy even the panties in that set of lingerie.

At the beginning of the second semester, she noticed a small typewritten card, newly thumbtacked to the bulletin board at the post office:

MODELS WANTED
COMMUNITY OUTREACH
LIFE STUDIES CLASS
EVENINGS
$10/HOUR
SEE B. TRENT
ART DEPT.

Studying the words, she imagined herself wearing the plaid skirt from Smyth's as she took her seat in the course for which she had just registered — American History Since the Civil War. Then she saw herself, quietly, so as not to wake her still-sleeping roommate, removing the tassel loafers from their sheath of tissue in the box on the first morning she'd wear them to breakfast. Carefully, Suzanne untacked the notice and slipped both card and tack into her jacket pocket.

The next afternoon she found Assistant Professor William Trent in his office at the back of Converse Hall. Since Trent had taught no freshman classes in the first semester, no one on Suzanne's hall had encountered him; she'd heard nothing about him. Later, she learned that the art majors talked about him constantly. He was from San Francisco; he was a renegade on the faculty; he was always challenging the Hollins way of doing things; he spent a lot of time chatting up the maids and janitors who worked for the college; and he probably wasn't going to get tenure. Most afternoons, he worked at his sculpture outside, in an area the college had allotted to him on the edge of the parking lot. He used welding equipment. Back there, he had set up a pulley-and-lever apparatus that enabled him to maneuver chunks of steel, weirdly shaped and perforated sheets of iron, sections of underpass pipe, chrome spangles, and monstrous chains. Professor Trent had been observed working there with his shirt off, very skinny and hairy, unusually so, in fact, and visibly glistening with sweat.

At his office doorway Suzanne stood, waiting for the professor to look up from whatever it was he was doodling with on his desk. "Hi," she finally said.

"Classes full," he said, his head still bent. "No room."

It irked her that he wouldn't look at her. His hair was long, thick, dark, and curly, but with his head bowed like that, she couldn't see much of his face. So she stepped inside the office, took the card from her jacket pocket, and set it, with an audible snap, directly in front of him on the desk. Then she stepped back. This was bold of her, she knew; it was only because of his rudeness that she'd done it. Every other faculty member and staff person she'd encountered at the college had been so elaborately polite that she felt righteous in confronting him.

Trent didn't move his head, but she could tell that he'd shifted his eyes to the card. "I wondered why I wasn't getting any responses," he said. Then he looked up.

She felt as if she'd gasped, though she was pretty certain she'd made no sound. She hoped not. What she had to reckon with was a swarthy, sharp-featured, high-cheekboned, thin-lipped, three-days-unshaven, and gaunt face of such vividness that Suzanne felt mildly assaulted by it. Did the man mean to wound her with the intensity of his stare? His large eyes made the stare abrasive — they were such deep brown as to be nearly black, and because they were so large, they gave the impression of having been manufactured, as if Professor Trent's real eyes had been replaced with glass ones. But he could see; she could tell that instantly. The man could definitely see.

"You took it, didn't you?" he said, his voice soft, his lips curling in amusement.

"What?" Suzanne said. She was grateful that her powers of speech hadn't wholly deserted her.

"The card." Trent picked it up and held it out to her. "My ad."

She said nothing. She was answering his ad in a proper way. He was the one being rude, first by not looking at her, and now, being doubly rude by assessing her in an insinuating manner. She made herself meet his stare.

"Any experience?" he asked, his voice still soft.

"What?" she said.

He wiggled the card.

She got what he meant — experience at modeling — but she didn't like his fanning the card at her.

She shook her head.

Again, he curled his lips. "Good. Come tomorrow night. Up in the main studio — 204 Converse. Eight o'clock sharp. Come early so that I can set you up."

She waited, thinking he would tell her more, but he broke off and bowed his head over the sheet of doodles on the desk. He might as well have said, "Dismissed."

She turned to go.

"You want to be my only model? You've got it." But the murmured words didn't seem directed at her. It was as if he'd accidentally spoken aloud something that crossed his mind.

Suzanne paused only a moment before walking quickly out of the building. Trent was — this was something girls on her hall said frequently and casually, though Suzanne herself had hardly *thought* the word before — an asshole. The rest of that day she was certain she wouldn't show up the next night. But when she woke the next morning, she knew she would. And when she presented herself to him at five minutes before eight, B. Trent — which was how she'd come to think of him — didn't even say hello; he started telling her what she was to do.

"Like this," he said. And with his lanky body, he demonstrated poses. She was to change position every fifteen minutes. B. Trent was "setting her up" as the students began filtering into the big room. "This one's the easiest," he said, "because you'll be tired at the end of the hour. That's why it's like this — straight on, totally relaxed, let your head come forward so that you're looking at the floor directly in front of you. You don't have to look at anybody out there. Adjust your weight, even though you're standing still. Shift so that you've got it first on one foot, then on the other, and then on your butt propped up against the stool." He smacked the seat of the stool like the backside of a horse. "Okay?" He stepped nearer, caught her eye, and spoke softly enough not to be heard even by the nearest student. "This is nothing," he said. "Don't make a big deal out of it. It's just work. People have been doing it for hundreds of years. Men and women."

Suzanne nodded. She couldn't imagine that she was going to

do what he'd said. Maybe she would. Although standing in front of people with her clothes off seemed like something from a dream, she wasn't sure how she felt about it. And there was nothing to keep her from saying, "I guess I can't do it after all," and walking her body right out the door of 204 Converse Hall.

"There's a screen over there." B. Trent nodded toward the far corner. "A place to hang your clothes. A robe, too, in case you didn't bring your own." He was obviously trying to size her up, figure out how she was going to do. This last pose, facing the class, propped against the stool, with her feet apart, like John Wayne waiting for the bad guy to draw his pistol — could she show herself like that to twenty-five people?

"They're all grown-ups," he said quietly. "You're nothing they haven't seen before."

He wore not particularly clean jeans and an untucked denim shirt; no wonder he thought it didn't matter whether she kept her clothes on or took them off. But at least he was being considerate. And he was maybe the thinnest healthy man she'd ever seen. It was interesting that a man so careless of his appearance could still be a professor of art.

B. Trent again nodded toward the screen, and Suzanne walked over to it.

She guessed she was lucky in never having had to think much about her body. As far as she knew, it wasn't exceptional in any way — "standard issue," her father would have said if she'd asked him. Both he and Suzanne's mother had waged a campaign to convince her and her sisters, as they grew up, that they were regular people, average citizens. "Don't go thinking you're so special, missie," they liked to say, especially to her. She was always the one in danger of violating the family ethic. The effusive teachers' comments that accompanied Suzanne's report cards tended to make her parents quarrelsome at dinnertime. "We're just your basic citizens around here, young lady. You get no special privileges," they'd say when she requested permission to join the Debate Club or take part in any afterschool activity. "Is somebody trying to get above her raising?" her mother would ask, arching her eyebrow. Lately, in the general liberation of her first year at Hollins, Suzanne had begun to gauge how oppressive her upbringing was. But in this one regard, she supposed it was good. Nobody in her home had ever made a fuss, positive or negative, about her body or her appearance, so she'd grown up afflicted with neither vanity nor shame. As she undressed behind the screen in the corner of 204 Converse Hall and looked down at her body after removing her clothing, she gave a little grin toward her chest and stomach. "Nothing special here," she whispered, then slipped on the robe, took a deep breath, and stepped out from behind the screen.

"Try this," B. Trent said, stepping up on the platform with her. She felt a rush of adrenaline as he came toward her. Because the students were quiet, she'd quickly lost her awareness of being looked at. She was alone under the hot light, her mind drifting in a slipstream of memory and fantasy, a little movie of herself going home for spring break, walking into the house, and watching her sisters' faces as they noticed her new shoes. Suddenly B. Trent was kneeling beside her, adjusting her leg, his hand pressing the back of her knee. "Unlock this," he told her. "You can't keep your knees locked for a long time, or you'll cripple yourself." He was smiling up at her as he pressed the back of her knee with one hand and clasped the other around her ankle.

Letting the knee unlock, she couldn't keep from grunting with the pain that jolted up her thigh.

"Sorry, I should have warned you about that," B. Trent said

softly. "Got to give the old joints a little slack." He stood up. "Here, let's try this." And with a hand at her elbow and an arm around her back, he guided her to the stool. "Put your feet here," he said, bending and grasping her ankle to lift her foot onto the rung of the stool. "Other one, too," he whispered. "Just let those legs relax and straighten your back." He put a hand against the small of her back and pushed slightly. Then he stepped around in front of her and placed one hand on each of her shoulders, pressing her upward. "Look straight at me," he murmured. "That's right. Just like that. Okay?" He looked at her face, keeping his hands on her shoulders as if he had to hold her in place lest she slump down into boneless, muscleless ignominy. And there was that half-smile curling at the corners of his mouth; he was as close to her face as the lady who cut her hair. What she wanted to say right at that moment was "You know, you could shave a little more often."

He moved away and glanced at the clock. "Only one more position after this one. Make it easy on yourself. Whatever you feel like." And he stepped off the platform to move from one student to the next, all at work with their sketch pads. She heard the murmur of his voice as he commented and offered suggestions.

It was easy enough to sit still on the stool. Too easy. She could sense the students viewing her as merely an object they were to draw. But she was embarrassed that B. Trent thought she couldn't endure the discomfort of that fourth position. She was riled up in a way she couldn't account for, as if she were unable to recall a dream that reverberated in her consciousness. She had an urge to do something, shout or launch into a speech or stand up and walk out of the room, leaving her clothes behind — something to shock this roomful of ridiculously silent and somber would-be Rembrandts.

She heard B. Trent clear his throat. When she let her eyes locate him out in the classroom, she saw that he was staring at the clock. So she'd spaced out on the time. All right, so what? Setting her feet on the floor, she experienced a rush of vertigo and had to steady herself with both hands on the stool before she could take up the last of the positions. He materialized beside her. Maybe the man was skinny, but at the moment he seemed almost a giant, too wide and too tall to be standing so close to her. "You okay?" he said.

She started to say, *Don't touch me,* which is when she realized what had upset her. It was his hands on her a few minutes ago. She started to say it again: *Don't touch me.* But part of her stopped the words before they reached her throat. "I'm fine," she said.

She let him help her into the last position.

In the days that followed, Suzanne admitted to herself that she had a secret. It wasn't by design, and she supposed she could change it in an instant. All she had to do was talk to Sarah, her roommate, about her job modeling for the life studies class. Sarah would have paid rapt attention — and it would be nice, talking about B. Trent with Sarah. But Sarah might mention the matter to Elizabeth, her friend across the hall, and soon Suzanne's modeling job would be a topic of public discussion. What she wasn't sure she could talk about with anybody was the part that weighed on her mind — B. Trent's hands, the way he put his hands on her.

She knew it was improper. He shouldn't touch her like that — as if she were an object that he could manipulate any old way he wanted to. The more she thought about it, the more appalled she became. In the week following that first evening, especially when she stayed up late studying, she found herself making speeches to the man. And as she became exhausted from her schoolwork, the language of her imagined tirades became irate. But on two different mornings, when her alarm clock woke her, she had a delicious sense of having been with B. Trent in some warm, dark place, of their having talked for hours and then curling up to sleep together, his body wrapped around hers, his arms over her shoulders, his hands cupping hers in a pocket of darkness right in front of her nose and mouth. It was a memory of such deep pleasure that on both mornings she resisted waking, stopped the alarm, and tried to dip back down into sleep.

Suzanne was barely eighteen years old. That she had had no experience with love embarrassed her. She'd never told Sarah or anyone at Hollins that through her whole four years of high school, she had experienced nothing more than a brief crush on a boy. She *could* probably confess to Sarah that she was a virgin and even tell her that, before she came to Hollins, she hadn't been on more than a couple of dates. She could blame it on growing up in Stevens Creek and on the overprotectiveness of her parents. But that she hadn't ever felt *anything* for anybody? Maybe that was — evidence of what? Of her being romantically and sexually crippled? After she'd been at Hollins for only a month or two, she learned that several senior female professors, austere and brilliant ladies, lived by themselves in the little houses on Faculty Lane, and it occurred to her that at the age of eighteen, they may have been much like her — too smart to have normal lives. Maybe they, too, in high school, had only tepidly experienced romance or desire. Now they were surrounded and admired by colleagues and students, but they went home at the end of each day to an empty house. Or to their research. Maybe that's what they went home to every day: their research. The thought of such a life made her shiver.

During the week after her first night of modeling, Suzanne didn't catch sight of B. Trent. She could have, but only if she went out of her way. He didn't eat in the dining hall; he didn't frequent the snack bar; she'd never seen him in the library. It was as if he were a troll who lived on the underside of the campus at the rear of Converse Hall. If she had seen him, she might have had fewer misgivings about showing up for the eight o'clock class on Wednesday evening. She imagined all sorts of ways B. Trent might humiliate her. He could give her that arrogant smile and tell her he'd found someone else to model for the life studies class, somebody who knew what she was doing and didn't need him to nurse her through the evening's work. In fact, the more she thought about it, the more certain she was that the evening would be humiliating. She knew she'd blush when she saw him, though she had no idea what she'd say. She might lecture him on keeping his hands off his models or, as easily, confess that she'd had uncommonly pleasing dreams about him. By 7:45 on Wednesday evening, when she stepped through the door of 204 Converse Hall, she felt as if she were running a high fever.

"I was wondering if you'd come back. How you doing?" B. Trent was neither grinning nor frowning. He was sitting on the platform, facing the door, speaking directly to her. Of course he wasn't waiting for her, but just for a moment she had the flighty thought that maybe he was. He wore the same clothes he'd worn the previous week — the denim shirt so rumpled that it looked as if he'd slept in it every night since the last time she'd seen him. "Good thing you did come," he said, "or I'd have had to pose for them myself."

She didn't know whether he was teasing her or was serious.

"Guess it's been done before, teacher modeling for the students. Not sure I'm the man to bring it off, though. Probably confuse everybody. Have to try it sometime before they kick me out of this place. Rather do it for one of the daytime classes, though. What would your classmates say about their professor being the model for his drawing classes?"

What track was he on? How was she supposed to know whether he wanted to discuss this or was off on some dumb idea that had just occurred to him. She shook her head.

He let a beat go by and tilted his head at her. "Do you speak English?"

"What?"

"I think that's the only word you've ever said to me. 'What.' You may have said it three times now, and it's the only thing I've heard you say. So it occurred to me that maybe English isn't your first language."

She couldn't help herself; she laughed out loud. Which she knew was wrong, because B. Trent had intended only a little sarcasm. But what made it so funny was that he — who had been so vivid in her thoughts — didn't have the slightest idea of who she was!

"You don't even know my name, do you?" she asked.

"I'm sorry, I don't."

"Suzanne Yarborough." She extended her hand. And now she was the one with an edge to her words. She took the hand he raised — and its calluses shocked her. No wonder she'd been sensitive to his touch on her shoulders, the back of her knee, her ankle, the small of her back.

"Bill Trent," he said. She could see a twitch at each corner of his mouth, where his smile was about to appear. But at that moment two students stepped into the classroom — and she recognized them as men who worked in the dining hall kitchen. So that's what B. Trent was up to — holding classes for college employees. She'd have given herself over to admiring him, except for the quickness with which he broke away from his handshake. Instead, she returned to being irked. She understood that he had decided to treat her as if she were a veteran model and to give her no more attention than necessary. After the handshake, he didn't glance at her any more than politeness demanded.

Gradually Suzanne realized that she had an abnormal awareness of B. Trent; it was as if she were wired to him. She knew where he was in the room; she could hear his sonorous baritone murmuring suggestions to this student, then the next. She felt each of his glances up toward her pose under the lights, checking the exact angle of what the student was trying to draw.

Suddenly he was there again, right beside her — as though he'd flown up to the platform — and now he was moving her body around like a mannequin in a store window. At least he was talking to her while he adjusted her position, because otherwise she could not have tolerated what he was doing with these bricklayer's hands of his; she would have screamed. But his voice made it all right; it was soothing as he steadily spoke to her. "Let's put this foot around here — good, now, if you don't mind, try leaning back in the other direction. That's right. And can you move your arm away from your torso a little? I want them to try articulating the ribcage. That's right; that's very good; thank you very much."

Then he was gone, flown off the platform and into the classroom, and though his abrupt leaving felt like a cold draft on her skin, her invisible connection with him seemed all the more amplified. It was as if she could hear what he was saying down there to her left — "Use the side of your hand like this to smudge in the shadows. See, there, how it's done?" — even though she knew he was almost whispering. And in her mind, she could see his hand as he brushed the heel of that half-fist on the drawing. A wave of dizziness washed lightly over her when she caught herself matching her breathing to his. She knew that was her imagination, but the knowledge didn't help her put a stop to it.

Again he appeared beside her, or, rather, behind her, with his hands on her shoulders now, very firm, and gently turning her. "That's right, around this way, please. Now, if you'll raise your arms like this, yes, both of them up this way. I know it won't be comfortable, and I won't make you stand this way very long."

When he came around her and stood close, she could feel the edges of his clothing touch her skin. That was when the tremors started. With her arms in the grip of those rough palms, her torso turned hot and cold at the same time.

She had no control.

She knew he'd figured it out the instant he glanced down at her ridiculously tightened nipples. Suzanne had only one wish — that she be struck dead.

For a fraction of an instant, because the sensations at work in her mind and body were so intense, she believed that she might be granted mercy and ascend into her good death right there in 204 Converse Hall, in front of the life studies class.

Because it didn't happen, her next wish was that B. Trent not let go of her arms. The shock in his face was telling her he was about to do that, let go of her and back away from her body to stand gaping at her.

If he did that, she'd bolt, naked or not, from the classroom and not stop running until she got back to the dormitory.

He didn't. His grip had loosened, but he caught her up again, higher, more by the shoulders now, holding her almost too tight, maintaining the distance between their bodies, but shifting the two of them so that she was shielded from the view of most of the students. She and he stood alone in a small pocket of space while he helped her brace herself against the stool.

Then he stayed in front of her for the time it took her to breathe normally. He said nothing, and though she didn't look at his face, she was certain it displayed concern — maybe *horrified* concern — as if she'd been having a seizure. Well, maybe that was a way to think of it. But she knew he knew what it was.

"Sorry," he murmured.

"Not your fault," she replied in a cracked voice.

Then she risked an upward glance and saw those big eyes taking her in and that too-expressive mouth showing involuntary bemusement. But at least he had the grace not to say anything else. He let go of her shoulders, turned to the class, and announced, "Break time, folks. We need a little break here." And with his arms spread wide, he herded the students away from her and out of the room like cattle.

So she was, in the long run, grateful to him. In the short run, however, she got the hell off the platform and behind the screen and into her clothes and out of the classroom and, not quite running but briskly making her way, through the gatherings of chatting students in the hall and out into the cold clear night air. Pulling that air into her lungs as she walked up the hill toward the center of the campus, she heard B. Trent's voice calling out, "Hey! Hey, Miss Yarborough!" He didn't even know what to call her. And that's when she started running at full speed back to the dormitory, clutching her wadded-up robe like a football against her chest.

For two days, the memory was like an illness — his hands on her and her fall over the edge into black space. Obsessively, she played through those eight or nine minutes again and again. And she was relieved when she finally received a plain envelope, with her name and mailbox number on it, containing three twenty-dollar bills and a handwritten — or, rather, handprinted — note:

Miss Yarborough,

The students chip in to pay for their models. We're a volunteer operation, and that's why this is not a check from the college. I guess you're not coming back, so this seems about what we owe you.

If you'd like to talk sometime, I'm usually at the gym every morning during the breakfast hour. Neutral territory, you know. The only people there then are the janitors.

Bill Trent

She decided to go the next morning. She dreaded it, but she knew she had to put the experience behind her. And now that he'd made her think of it, she worried about running into him on campus without first having talked to him. Had she been in high school, she'd have taken pains to avoid him. But this was college — she had to *try* to be stronger. So she got up earlier than usual, dressed carefully, and prepared herself.

When she stepped through the lobby and into the brightly lit gymnasium, there he was, a lone figure bamming a basketball against the floor and moving quickly across the expanse of gleaming wood. She had to blink against the light. Coming her way, he reached the top of the key, pulled up, and took his jump shot. The ball bounced off the rim, but he was already rising toward it, snatching the rebound, and putting up the ball again. This time it richocheted off the rim and back toward the center of the court. He let it bounce back in the other direction as he trotted over to her. He was breathing hard; his face was flushed; and he radiated a smell that nearly made her take a step back. In his tie-dyed T-shirt, old Bermuda shorts, and high-top tennis shoes, he cut a ridiculous figure, especially in the grandly vacant space and the light that was blasting down on them from the high windows on every side of the gym. The man still needed a shave and a decent haircut, but he seemed so pleased with himself that he looked years younger. "Hey," he said, grinning.

She nodded. She was grinning, too, though that wasn't how she'd planned to act. When she decided to come, she expected to carry out a sober conversation, in which she would explain that she hadn't been herself that evening in 204 Converse, and that he shouldn't believe her behavior showed who she really was. Also, she wanted to say that he should give thought to how he worked with the models for his students. Maybe she'd have had the courage to tell him he ought to keep his hands to himself.

Now, however, something about the empty gymnasium, all the light and open space — not to mention the simple smiley-face of B. Trent — wouldn't let her proceed with the plan she'd rehearsed while walking over here. "You do this every morning?" she heard herself ask. She swept her hand out toward the open floor to distract him from the smile she couldn't control.

"Keeps me sane," he said. "In high school, I never could make the team. Over here, I'm first-string varsity. I play every minute of every game, and my team hasn't lost one yet. You play basketball, Miss Yarborough?"

Suzanne laughed out loud. At Blue Ridge High School, every year the gym teachers had jokingly threatened to fail her in phys ed because she was such a hopeless athlete. "Basketball is about the last thing on my list," she said. "I guess it must be the first thing on yours."

B. Trent didn't answer. He widened his maniacal grin and trotted onto the vast floor to fetch the ball from the far end of the court. As he picked it up, he broke into a full run, turned in a wide arc back toward her, and dribbled the ball, faking and weaving as he ran. He wasn't especially graceful, but watching him move made her giddy. She could imagine him as a crazy kid alone on a playground, his skinny legs and arms pumping along, his long hair flying out behind him as he ran. She laughed as she watched the grown man. How could someone who'd taken over her thoughts be so comical? In her amusement — which she took as an intended gift from B. Trent — she suddenly felt gloriously free of him.

"Here you go!" he shouted as he approached. He gave her a soft bounce pass that popped the ball up perfectly in front of her. She couldn't help pulling her hands out of her jacket pockets to catch it. Surprised that she managed to hold on to it, she laughed still louder.

B. Trent kept running in a tighter circle away from her and back along the top of the key. "Now back to me!" he shouted. "Here you go, Miss Yarborough, right here." He clapped his hands so that somehow she knew exactly how to bounce the ball to him, even though her pass was clumsy, and he caught it at the instant he left his feet to rise toward the basket for an easy lay-up.

It ended as such a completely flubbed shot that he took a pratfall beneath the backboard and then put on a silly face as he sat there, shouting, "That was your fault! That pass was late getting to me."

"My fault!" she yelled. She trotted onto the floor after the ball. "My fault!" she said as she ran it down. "I'll show you what's my fault!" she shouted as she flung the ball at him.

It was a classic girl throw; she knew it as the ball left her hands. He had to pitch his body sideways and stretch, but he did manage to catch it. "Good pass," he said, sitting up straight. "You make the team. You're in. You didn't know you were so cool, did you?"

Their laughter was rising up toward the ceiling when the door nearest them opened with a clang. There stood Miss

Palmer, head of the Phys Ed Department, surrounded by the light, as if a thunderbolt had brought her down from the clouds to witness the antics of these foolish mortals. "I thought I heard someone in here," she said. She looked first at Suzanne and then at B. Trent.

Silence folded around them. Suzanne could tell that neither Miss Palmer nor B. Trent knew what to say, nor, certainly, did she. But she knew that, as weird as the situation might appear, she was doing nothing wrong, and neither was B. Trent. Not that Miss Palmer had accused them of anything or expressed disapproval in her voice, but she was, perhaps, the most formidable senior faculty member on campus. For nearly forty years she had lived alone in one of the little ranch houses on Faculty Row. Her demeanor was almost always intimidating — she seemed to strive for a gruff appearance — and the moment did hold a certain dramatic content. In her dark coat, with her brilliant scarlet scarf rising from her collar, Miss Palmer stood still, with her eyes focused on the middle distance. It was as if she were considering what was appropriate for her to say and do about the situation, a woman student alone with a young male professor in her gymnasium.

By a downward flick of Miss Palmer's eyes, Suzanne was reminded that she had put on her new tassel loafers to walk over here this morning. She had had misgivings about spending her modeling money on those shoes at Davidson's yesterday afternoon, and even more misgivings about wearing them for her "talk" with B. Trent. But they went well with her good gray-and-navy kilt and her best cable-knit sweater. With their leather heels and soles, the loafers were obviously the wrong shoes to wear on the polished wooden floor of Miss Palmer's gymnasium. Suzanne felt herself blush. How could the lady not say something about such a violation?

Miss Palmer's eyes moved back toward B. Trent, sitting with the ball on his lap and his legs straight out before him. Though he looked directly back at her, he was clearly going to say nothing by way of explanation until she demanded he do so. And in Suzanne's eyes, B. Trent could hardly have appeared more inappropriate — hairy, skinny, absurdly dressed, and male as a jock strap.

Miss Palmer's attention swiveled back to Suzanne, who took a deep breath to ready herself for the chastisement that was certain to come.

"Are you all right, my dear?"

Suzanne was startled. Was the woman worried about her safety? Surely not, but what else could Miss Palmer mean? "I'm fine, ma'am," she managed to answer.

"All right, then," Miss Palmer said with a nod. And though it wasn't a smile, there came to her face the most benevolent expression Suzanne had ever beheld on a real person's face. In later years, after she'd become an art historian, she realized that she'd recognized the expression from religious paintings — by Giotto and Raphael, maybe — reproductions of which she may have seen during her years in Stevens Creek. "Yes, my dear," Miss Palmer murmured. "I can see that's exactly what you are." And she walked out, letting the door swing shut behind her.

V

JACK NELSON was smitten with the sound of Elly Jacobs's voice from the first words he heard her utter — "You don't work for the university? You're my first Burlington townie, Mr. Nelson." She shook his hand and gave him a wry smile. "How do you do?" There was a conspiratorial tinge to her voice, along with a faint Southern accent and a contralto warmth in the little melodies of her sentences. Suzanne had just introduced them to each other at the welcoming reception in Waterman Manor — a zoo of an event that ordinarily Jack would have fled as soon as possible. But that evening, long after Suzanne had drifted away to mingle with her colleagues, Jack stood beside the new assistant professor of studio art, asking her questions, listening, and taking pleasure in the sound of her voice. From then on, whenever department social events brought them together, that's what Jack would do — seek her out and encourage her to talk.

And later, after she'd joined the Halvorson's String Quartet, Elly charmed Jack with her account of how the group was started. It took its name from a downtown restaurant where Mac Delgado, first violinist and founding member, waited tables. Halvorson's was also where Caroline Wadhams, cellist and founding member, had lunch every Thursday with her mother and sister. On those noontime occasions, in spite of the age difference (she was near fifty; he was twenty-six), Caroline and Mac carried on sufficient chitchat over the seatings, the menus, the drink orders, the checks, and so on, to learn of their mutual background and passion. One day, on a whim, as the ladies were about to depart, Mac suggested that he and Caroline should try playing some duets. Caroline agreed and invited Mac to her mother's house, on Willard Street, that coming Sunday afternoon at two o'clock. A single run-through of Haydn's Duet for Violin and Cello in C Major convinced the two of them that they were born to play chamber music together. Caroline was all precision and exacting musicianship; Mac was pure expressiveness and fluid extravagance. He was freedom; she was discipline. Musically, each was the perfect complement to the other. That esthetic tension between Mac and Caroline was the character of the Halvorson's String Quartet.

Elly, who was the second violinist, conveyed the story to Jack Nelson after they'd become close. She knew he liked listening to her and her stories. She told him she never saw herself as of the same caliber as Mac or Caroline, and was grateful to them for allowing her to be a member of the Halvorson's. As far as Jack knew, that was Elly's single area of humility. Though she loved the violin, and had a gift for it, she'd never taken her musical talent seriously. Her passion, from the time she was twelve, had been art history. When she was twenty-seven, the University of Texas Press published her dissertation on Mary Cassatt. A few years later, here she was, teaching at the University of Vermont. Knowledgeable people — including Jack — understood that UVM was merely a stopping point along the way in Elly Jacobs's ultimate journey to Harvard, Stanford, or Yale. She wasn't obnoxious about it, but the only people Elly truly respected in Burlington were Mac Delgado and Caroline Wadhams. She loved what she called the "asymmetry of their stories."

As a twenty-year-old, Mac had got caught selling hash, which was how he'd been supporting himself as a student at Juilliard. His parents hired him a good lawyer; the lawyer found him a lenient judge; so Mac spent only a short time in jail. But the conviction was on his record. It was also "engraved in his musical soul," Elly assured Jack. "He doesn't care," she explained, "about the literal text of the score, even though he understands it perfectly. He brings a jazz sensibility to chamber music. He never plays anything the same way twice. And yet it's never so far from the score that it violates his contract with the other players. He knows, almost intuitively, how the rest of us want to play the piece; then he subtly moves us into his own interpretation. Mac is an outlaw, all right — a genius of an outlaw. I've never played with anybody like him."

Caroline Wadhams, on the other hand, was the ultimate grown-up good girl. She was a tall woman, thick-bodied, with short springy gray hair and wire-rimmed glasses, which, when she played, slid to the tip of her nose. Cello, she once told Elly, was what kept her alive. Her father had given her her first lessons while she sat in his lap. He had also founded the one-person bookkeeping firm that Caroline successfully maintained. She confided to Elly that few things in life bored her as much as accounting, but apparently she could carry out the activity with only ten percent of her attention. It was no surprise to Caroline that Elly was a scholar and university professor; she assumed that Elly's attitude toward teaching must be the same as hers toward bookkeeping. What Caroline didn't get about Elly, however, was her love life. Caroline had never had a serious romantic interest. "Except for my father," she told Elly, laughing. "If it hadn't been for my mother, I could have happily married him."

Elly Jacobs had been through a couple of husbands by the time she first arrived in Burlington. "Men fail," she explained to Jack. "That has to be the guiding principle for any woman hoping to achieve romantic sanity. Accepting it was hard, but now that I've broken through, I can't understand why it isn't obvious to everyone. A woman takes it personally when a husband or a lover lets his eyes slide along in the direction of the blonde with pretty legs and a short skirt. The man doesn't mean it as a personal comment; it's how the apparatus works. My first husband was especially vulnerable to cleavage. He couldn't keep himself from staring at any woman who aired the tops of her boobies in public. That used to make me cry. We'd go out to dinner; I'd notice he was sweating. When I glanced behind me, I'd see some woman displaying her chest. I'd weep; he'd apologize. I wish I had him back, the poor guy. Compared with my second husband, Bobby was a cherub, an absolute cherub."

Elly was from Texas and had a gift for narrative. Her students loved her. She'd throw a slide of a painting up in front of the class and start talking about it. Kids who didn't know a Warhol from a Botticelli showed up for her lectures. If she was good in the classroom, she was great sitting naked in her apartment bed, with the covers teepeed around her and a glass of chilled white wine in her hand.

"My second husband was abysmally criminal," she explained to Jack one afternoon. "He teaches film at Reed College, but if they ever catch on to what he's actually up to, he'll be teaching a cellmate how to play solitaire. He's put together this course in pornography and is daring the administration to shut it down.

Liberal principles, the sacred nature of the classroom, art from unexpected sources, all that garbage — he's ready to lay the whole shmear on them, and they know it. But what he really gets off on is watching freshman girls' faces the first time they get a look at a hard-core bondage flick. White panties; that's what the man's into. White cotton panties and thirteen-year-old girls chewing bubblegum. The man is warped, and the man is a genius for having figured out how to do his sick little routines and, instead of ending up in prison, earning himself a handsome salary. You want to know how he got to me? It's my first year of teaching, at Reed. I'm sitting in the faculty dining room, books all around me, notebook open, and pen frantically scratching notes for my two o'clock lecture. The man, whom I've never seen before, saunters up, confident as Beelzebub, and sits down at my table. Sunglasses, beard, tweed jacket, black turtleneck, turquoise earring, cup of herb tea — which he sets on top of my two-hundred-dollar catalogue of the Whitney permanent collection.

"'Miss — is it Jacobs?' he asks, and I nod. 'Miss Jacobs,' he says again, clearing his throat. 'You have a serious body. Not a profound body, but a serious one.'

"People are all around us. I figure I can slap the sunglasses off the jerk's face, or try to find out where he's coming from. 'Maybe you don't know the difference between serious and profound, mister,' I tell him. 'About that I won't presume to make a judgment. There is, however, one statement I can make with confidence, and that is that you don't know jackshit about my body.'"

"So I gather up my books and my notes, and I'm turning toward the exit when he murmurs, 'All right, profound, then. Have it your way.'

"I like the moment. I go back to the table and set down my

books. 'That's more like it.' A month later the two of us are standing in front of a justice of the peace."

Jack understood that Elly's story was only an approximate version of the truth. No doubt her second husband was both better and worse than she made him out to be, but since he and Jack weren't likely ever to cross paths, Jack was happy to accept the version of him Elly presented — especially since Jack knew that compared with that guy, he looked like a prince.

Elly might have concentrated less on her teaching and writing and given more of her energy to the Halvorson's except for the fourth member, the violist, Patricia Magistrale, Mac Delgado's girlfriend. Elly couldn't stand "that girl," as she called her. But Elly could never make a case against her, except the obvious one: that Patty Magistrale always appeared to be lost in a deep, dense fog. Jack figured that Patty's lost quality was the main thing that appealed to Mac, because it appealed to him, too. Patty had these shoes she wore for the performances that you nearly had to laugh aloud at — brown crepe-soled oxfords she wore with black tights. The way she sat in her chair, leaning forward and squinting at her music, with her feet flat, pigeon-toed in front of her, made her look like a cartoon of a grade-schooler taking her first viola lesson. But that was Patty — always looking as if she didn't know the first thing. The fact was, she knew plenty — or certainly enough to survive any occasion. First glance at her, you thought the girl cut her own hair and bought her clothes at Sears. Second glance, you thought, *But she doesn't look bad.* Even when it came to the music, you thought, *My God, that girl can't possibly play Schumann.* Meanwhile, giving the appearance of sawing a two-by-four with a forsythia twig, she played with surpassing competence. To see Patty Magistrale perform with the Halvorson's Quartet was to witness a clumsy but successful struggle. Jack found her a dear girl to watch while she was playing. Which irked Elly all the more.

"Mac says she's the ideal violist. 'A classic role player,' he calls her," Elly said. "I've spent my entire life moving people like that out of my way. 'Role players!' The world is stuffed with 'role players.' We don't need one in the Halvorson's. Even in Burlington, Vermont, we could find a dozen violists who are better than that girl. I can't understand what Mac is thinking. She'd be happy as can be to go home with him and be his little role-playing girlfriend. Why does he need to have her in the quartet?"

Jack understood that Elly was engaging in rhetoric. When she was nervous before a performance, it calmed her to complain to him about Patty. What calmed her more was the carnal activity she carried on with Jack at her apartment an hour or so before she had to show up for a performance. For Elly, sex was an occasion to speak her mind — at length. Her daily life was full of distractions that kept her from concentrating on what she really wanted to talk about. When she and Jack got their clothes off and their bodies into the same bed, she could express what was on her mind. She was a tense and intense person, except after sex. More often than not, her climaxes included a little burst of weeping. Afterward, she became loose in body and spirit. "Look at these!" she'd say, puffing out her chest. "Are these the tits of a role player? I think not! These are the boobies of a kick-ass second violinist. Bobby was devoted to these, bless his heart." That was the mood she liked to be in when she set off to perform with the Halvorson's.

Jack had been happy enough to oblige Elly with her pre-performance rituals. Suzanne was serving as interim chairman of the Art Department. She was busy, distracted, and inclined to fall more frequently into those trances of hers — occasions when she sat so still for so long that Jack felt obliged to speak to her and bring her back to the present. And though she never said so, he could tell she didn't like him to do that. In general, Jack seemed to be in her way, bothering her with mundane matters she didn't want to deal with. Around Suzanne at home, he felt superfluous. Around Elly, he felt he was serving a purpose. He saw the arrangement as temporary and practical.

The one dangerous element was that Suzanne's interim chairmanship required her to conduct the two-year review of Elly's performance in the Art Department. Jack knew Elly was on Suzanne's mind a good deal — and in a troublesome way. Elly had little regard for her colleagues at UVM and little desire to remain at the university; she saw her job there as a way to pass the time until she finished her second book and had it published. Then she'd move on to a better job at a better university. She didn't consider the matter worth discussing; it was simply what was going to happen. Suzanne confided to Jack that she thought Elly was probably right about her future, but that it was wrong to allow her to condescend to the department. She thought Elly needed a scare.

"She's investing too much of her time and energy in that chamber group. I've been asked to convey that message to her," Suzanne told Jack on a rare evening when the two of them were having dinner at home. Jack had baked a salmon filet with a dill sauce and served it with cold asparagus salad, but Suzanne had neglected to compliment him on the meal. "What do you think?" she asked. "You've taken an interest in that Halvorson's group, haven't you? Do you think Elly will show the department some respect? Or will she dare us to send a negative recommendation to the dean?"

Had Suzanne been looking at Jack as she spoke, he would have taken her question as a sign that she knew what was going on between Elly and him. But she was gazing at her wineglass, as if hypnotized by the way it sparkled in the candlelight. In the twilight of their dining room, her dark hair made her pale skin almost a source of light itself. His wife was notably more attractive than Elly Jacobs, which at the moment struck him as peculiar. He admired Suzanne in deep ways that he knew didn't apply to Elly.

It came to Jack that the Halvorson's String Quartet had made him a little crazy. Listening to them made him feel better about his life. When he calculated how far out of his way he went to hear them perform, he knew he had become their one and only groupie. Of course he enjoyed watching Elly as she played. She was marvelous, with her body swaying and her face naked in its attention to the music. But he realized, too, that what absorbed him was watching all four players. Mac communicated with the three women by his facial expressions and his body movements. As soon as they began a piece, Caroline pasted on an unwavering smile probably intended to disguise her passion. Though her body moved only slightly, her fingers at the cello's neck did an expressive dance. And, of course, there was Patty, sawing away at her viola, squinting at her music as if she'd never seen it before, and sitting, flat-footed and stolid, like a tone-deaf beginner.

Most of all Jack loved the story of the quartet, how it began, the personalities of its members, and what the group might become, as well as who was thinking what of whom at every moment. The Halvorson's always seemed to him in danger of disintegrating. Would Elly lose her temper at Patty? Would Mac and Patty break up or Caroline decide she couldn't abide all the excess drama? Or would Mac lose his job at the restaurant and Elly quit the quartet to please the Art Department? But when they played the harmonious compositions of the eighteenth century, Jack entered a mood of cosmic permanence and well-being. In the sounds those four people made together by scraping horse-haired sticks against steel-strung wooden boxes was the possibility of beauty and deep human accord.

Of course Jack was neither a musician nor a particularly educated listener. As a child, growing up in Manhattan, he had had a few years of violin lessons and had played for a year in his middle school orchestra, but his life's work was in the business world, where, on a local scale, he was eminently successful. To himself Jack explained the intensity of his response to the Halvorson's as the fulfillment of his desire for exactitude in his daily life. Nothing in business ever worked out as it should. Compromising, altering the truth, and exploiting imperfection were basic principles of contemporary business practice, at least as far as his experience indicated. Here in town, Jack was an image maker and upgrader.

He knew Suzanne didn't like the work he did; once over dinner in a restaurant, she had blurted out, "Jack, how can you stand tricking people like that?" He told her he wasn't proud of it, but he was pretty certain it was what he'd been called to do, as she had been called to be a teacher and a scholar. She blushed when he said this. And though he didn't go on, he could have told her he was the best of his line in this part of the country. Everybody in Vermont knew that. Jack could take a furniture retailer whose primary motivation was greed, a man whose grandest dream was to own the most powerful motorboat on Lake Champlain, and, through publicity, transform him into an upright citizen of the community, a committed neighbor, and an advocate of the greater good. To put it bluntly, in direct proportion to his ability to capitalize on the least admirable human traits, Jack thrived. So he knew he was lucky to discover, in his middle age, the dimension of music — and to witness the coming-into-being of the Halvorson's String Quartet. He knew it was peculiar of him to think so, but he saw his intimacy with Elly Jacobs as a way of moving closer to the music, of becoming almost part of the group.

Why Elly had taken him as a lover was something he pondered only after the fact. This oversight embarrassed him, but he supposed it was a typical male foible. He knew that he rarely questioned his own desirability, though he suspected he was no better than the lowest specimens of his gender — balding, beergutted, hygienically retarded, semiliterate rednecks who envisioned themselves as enchanting to the opposite sex. A proper humility among males would no doubt put a halt to the evolution of the species. Imagining himself through Elly's eyes, Jack was the tanned and well-groomed man at a summer cocktail party who sat near the gazebo and listened to the quartet more attentively than anyone else. Jack was the cultivated gentleman at the first-night concert who asked intelligent questions about Boccherini. Jack was the tall fellow whose concentrated attention subtly informed Elly that he found her attractive. His early considerations of Elly's view of him omitted the fact that he was Suzanne Nelson's husband. Even before he'd introduced himself to her, Elly knew he was the spouse of her department chair. The one person who had some power over her — Suzanne — claimed Jack for a husband. That's why she took a sexual interest in him.

Margaret Wadhams, Caroline Wadhams's older sister, more or less on purpose, according to Elly, because of a rivalry that went back to Caroline's birth, arranged a scheduling conflict with a crucial Halvorson's rehearsal. She invited her bridge group to her mother's house for a Sunday afternoon, when the quartet usually rehearsed there. This particular week Mac Delgado was eager for the group to work on the third of the late Beethoven quartets, Opus 132, which he wanted to perform at the benefit concert for the Burlington Friends of Music. The piece would showcase his own abilities, but the viola part utterly baffled Patty Magistrale. One of Mac's basic principles was that he would never attempt to instruct Patty one-on-one for fear it would gum up their love life, so he needed Caroline to go over the piece with Patty. Caroline, however, because of an aversion to the idea of being a local music teacher — her mother had always hoped she would use her musical training by "giving lessons" — would help Patty only in the context of a full group rehearsal.

Elly Jacobs could have offered her apartment for the rehearsal, but this all happened during a week when she was profoundly irritated with Patty Magistrale and her Kleenex. Patty refused to perform without a box of Kleenex beneath her chair, because she suffered from allergies that often caused her nose to drip. Elly had lately been obsessing over the public image of the Halvorson's and how it was affected generally by Patty's appearance and specifically by Patty's box of tissues. At the end of the last rehearsal, she had asked Patty to seek other means of having her tissues available during the performances. Patty had looked Elly straight in the face and said, "Ms. Jacobs, if Ms. Wadhams or Mac asked me to do something for the quartet, I'd be happy to do it, because I respect them as artists. But I don't think I have to take any shit from you about my Kleenex." Carefully examining their instruments, the other two musicians sat in red-faced embarrassment, with Patty's words lingering in the air, until Elly cleared her throat and said, "All right, Ms. Magistrale. Make us look like a circus band if you want to."

Nevertheless, a place to rehearse had to be found, or Mac's dream of playing the Beethoven quartet would have to be forsaken. Even Elly, who considered the Kleenex discussion a personal humiliation, wanted Mac to have his Beethoven — but not enough to make her apartment available for the rehearsal.

"That girl may not enter my personal space," she told Jack during their Wednesday afternoon rendezvous. "I'm devoted to Mac, I love Beethoven, and I'm committed to the Halvorson's, but none of that means I have to pick up Patty Magistrale's used Kleenex from my apartment floor."

So Jack volunteered his house — which, of course, was also Suzanne's — for the rehearsal. It was a spontaneous offer, made when he and Elly were naked in her bed and he was enjoying Elly's amusing account of the Kleenex confrontation with Patty. But when Jack drove home that afternoon, he broke out in a sweat, wondering how to explain it to Suzanne — and how to justify offering the house before he'd checked with her. He and Suzanne were busy people; early in their married life, they had accepted the necessity of conferring with each other before making any social commitment. The invitation he had extended to the quartet was such a clear violation of their long-standing policy that even a spin master like himself was going to have trouble presenting it.

Two years pass. Vivienne by now has come to think of herself as a liar, and in moments of solitude the admission troubles her. "Old La Tour brought out the liar in me." She tests the idea one morning, lying on her back beneath her bedcovers. She loves nestling in her quiet reverie while her mother clangs cooking pans around in the kitchen downstairs. "La Tour got me to make things up. La Tour made me put together these little dreams." However, Vivienne cannot convince herself. Sadly, she admits that she is lying to herself about having lied to the old painter. He'd merely asked her questions to start her talking. The truth or the fiction of what she'd told him was of her own choosing.

Vivienne is seventeen — and known to be spoiled by her parents. Already the villagers think her too old to snare any of the best suitors in Lunéville's latest crop of potential husbands. She's not troubled; she knows these boys. She's confident there will be a husband for her when she gets around to choosing which one she wants. She has no doubt that whoever he is will be available. Vivienne recognizes a certain talent in herself. When, at around the age of five, she learned to control her facial expressions, boys began doing what she wanted. Often she didn't need to ask — an upward shift of her eyes could cause a boy to jump and grasp the branch of a cherry tree in order to offer her the cluster of fruit she desired. The slightest curling of a corner of her mouth could bring a boy to cut her a thick piece from his loaf of bread. In a box under her bed, Vivienne has a collection of toys and trinkets and good-luck charms that boys have given her over the years. It has been her policy not to turn down any gift unless something is suspicious about it or its giver.

Now her suspicion of herself interferes with the pleasurable thoughts that usually entertain her as she lies in bed. She is such a little liar! And almost no one knows it.

La Tour, of course, knows — La Tour, who is so old that she shudders when she thinks of him now. La Tour, to whom not so long ago she was closer than to her mother or father. La Tour, who finally showed her what was behind her shoulder. Wasn't he calling to her when she ran from his studio? Didn't she hear those words — *Come back!* — faintly voiced from his studio while she furiously put on her clothes in the courtyard?

Vivienne smiles grimly. Evidently her thoughts are beckoning her to walk through the village and visit the old painter. More clearly than a dream, she can see it: the journey she took each morning. But it surely isn't something she wants to do. La Tour, after all, saw her naked. Old as he is, feeble, almost entirely given over to death — a frog in the mouth of a snake — he'll want to see her that way again. Vivienne knows. "My dear, you must pose for me a few moments before you go. You must give me inspiration." That is how he will propose it to her.

A picture flashes into her mind and makes her sit up in bed: it is as clear as if she were standing before it. She feels blood heat move in her body. That painting belongs to her far more than to old La Tour! It began, it went on for almost a year, and it ended with the explosion of her seeing the canvas immediately after he'd completed the finishing touches. At times, all those hours — standing or sitting in silence or quiet conversation — seem like a long tale recited by her about herself. Vivienne climbs out of bed, pulls off her nightshirt, pours half a pitcher of water into her basin, and splashes it on her face. In a moment her mother will call her down to help in the kitchen.

During the months that she posed for La Tour, she had such high regard for him it was as if he were the king and she the lowest maidservant in his castle. She was fifteen then. Had La Tour asked her to bathe his feet, she would have happily done so. Now the idea makes her skin crawl.

There was a gradual progress to the picture. For weeks the old man talked with her as he sketched her in this pose and that, from this angle and that. They talked and talked. Vivienne realizes that it was in the old painter's studio that she grew out of her childhood. Until then, there had been only sporadic conversation between her mother and herself while they worked together in the house or in her father's shop. Her father, though garrulous with his customers, had little to say to his wife and daughter, even less than he wanted to hear from them. But La Tour — now there was a man who wanted talk to fill the air in his every waking moment. Vivienne smiles to remember how she spun her voice around him in great spirals of words and sentences. La Tour was the Great Questioner. When she seemed about to come to an end and she could think of nothing else to say, there was La Tour, firmly asking, "But, then, Vivienne, what did it look like? Can you describe how it smelled? What about the light? Tell me how the light entered the room." These conversations filled the studio while she posed and he sketched.

Then he began the picture. The memory makes Vivienne rub her shoulder. He gave her the yellow drapery that he had ordered from Paris especially for her, and every day she held it against her breasts. She asked one day whether she could take it home with her and wash it, because she'd made it dirty by holding it against herself for so many hours. She showed him the stains from her perspiring during the hot days. La Tour refused. The stains didn't matter. It was essential, he told her, that the color of the drapery remain exactly as it was. He couldn't risk its fading from being washed.

Today she knows that she — Vivienne — brought the painting into the world. La Tour did what he could do; he painted. But it was nothing for him. It was like putting on his clothes, eating his food, teasing his dogs. Painting was to him of no more consequence than is the mail to the horse that carries it from Nancy to Lunéville. Does the mail belong to the horse because it has made the journey? Of course not. And before Vivienne started coming to his studio, La Tour had stopped painting, it mattered so little to him. At her first visit to his studio, the old man had said, "Dear child, the last thing the world needs is another picture from the hand of La Tour." At the time, she thought he was making a modest joke. Now she understands that he said what he believed to be the truth.

If she goes to claim the painting as her own, La Tour will give it to her. This morning, as she stands facing the bare white wall of her bedroom, with water dripping from her face, she knows this with absolute certainty. First she will tell the old painter that he turned her into a liar. Next, she will explain that he is the one person in all of France whose advice she can trust on the problem of her lies. "At home," she will confess to him, "when Maman or Papa asks me a question, even about things that matter to no one, I tell a lie — or I think of a lie to tell. Sir, I curse myself for wanting to lie more than I want to tell the truth." La Tour will speak earnestly, and whatever he says will help; she is certain. Then she will inform him that the picture belongs to her. And, without arguing, he will agree. Most likely, he will merely nod and point toward the wall of his studio where the picture leans with others, a paint-spattered cloth protecting them from dust. "Take it," she can hear him whisper in his old man's rasping voice.

This morning Vivienne moves through her chores with unusual dispatch. Too late, she recognizes that she is making an impression on her mother. The deluded woman is chattering happily about the work they can accomplish this afternoon since they are getting so much done this morning — and so quickly! "I'm going into the village," Vivienne announces. Her mother stops what she is doing; her face reveals her feelings. She's hurt, but she's also curious. Although she won't ask Vivienne what her errand is, she'll maneuver the conversation in such a way as to encourage her daughter to confide in her. Vivienne sets herself to resist her mother's subtle efforts. She vows to herself that after she has retrieved her picture from La Tour and begun the cure for her lying, she will take up the project of selecting a husband. No husband could possibly be as stifling as this mother, who hangs over her shoulder in her every waking moment.

The afternoon is so bright and warm that, as she makes her way down the hill into town, Vivienne is transported back to the days of her childhood. Yet her exuberance is tinged with sadness. She wishes she could turn back time and be the charming child of the village, the shoemaker's daughter, the quaint and pretty girl whose parents protect her more than any Lunéville child has ever been protected. Vivienne can't help reaching her arm around her chest and touching her fingers to the back of her shoulder; the gesture has become a habit. When certain thoughts or moods come over her, she must reach behind to feel the coarse thatch. Today, she is embarrassed to catch herself doing it in public. *No wonder I'm a liar,* she admonishes herself. *I grew up hiding something I didn't know I was hiding.* As she walks, she tries out the notion that Maman and Papa are responsible for her lying ways, and it's such an attractive idea that it momentarily frees her from the disturbance she has felt all morning.

The recent lie that troubles her most severely is telling her parents that the hair on her back is disappearing. One evening at supper, by a circuitous sequence of observations, her father made it known that if she wanted, he would journey with her to Vézelise to consult a healer he had recently heard about, a man who reputedly could cure strange maladies. "Oh, it's started falling out, I think," Vivienne told him. She blurted out the sentence before thinking, but as she heard her words, she liked the idea and blithely went on. "In another six months, there won't be a trace; I'm outgrowing it."

Her mother's face took on such a glow of hope that Vivienne could say no more. She saw that her father, too, could barely restrain himself from cheering aloud at his daughter's news. The lie had made her parents happy, but it stings her to remember it. *I should have told them the hair was spreading, that in a few months my whole body and my face would be covered with it,* she thinks. A lie to hurt them was better than a lie that infected them with false hope.

Walking along the dusty, sunbathed village street, Vivienne

nods in appreciation of the bitter irony. During all the years of her childhood, before she went to see La Tour, her parents managed to keep her from knowing that a thatch of hair grew on her back. Now, during the years that have passed since she made her furious exit from La Tour's studio, she has managed to keep them from seeing the hair. She hides it from them as they hid it from her.

In fact, Vivienne acknowledges a peculiarity about herself. She likes her back — the way it is. If a magician or a healer offered to remove the hair back there, she would refuse. But she also understands that since her birth, Maman and Papa must have desperately yearned for it not to be so, for their daughter not to be marked as the odd one. The people of Lunéville are a superstitious lot; Vivienne's parents must have feared what could happen to their child if her marked shoulder became known in the village. She recognizes her lie to be especially mean in that it feeds her parents' deepest hopes. *They think I'll be able to marry without my husband running screaming from the house on our wedding night,* she thinks. And the idea of the fleeing husband amuses her.

Jack Nelson was one of the first men Suzanne had admired; her pattern was to feel contempt for a man soon after the initial interest. When she and Jack met, however, the contempt didn't arise on schedule, but she expected it any day. It was several months before she learned any details about his family. When she finally heard that his parents lived in Manhattan, on the Upper East Side, she figured that they were probably wealthy. So she decided that Jack was being modest about that, and she appreciated it. She did pry out of him that he'd graduated from the Choate School and attended Dartmouth for a couple of years before dropping out and eventually finishing at the University of Richmond.

The morning after he spent the first night in her apartment, she said, "I guess we're going to have to meet each other's family." The words sounded a lot more somber than she'd intended. They were sitting over coffee at the table in her tiny kitchen, she in her pajamas and Jack, showered but unshaven, in his wrinkled shirt. His jacket and tie were in the living room on a chair. Before she spoke, the two of them had been enjoying a companionable silence for some minutes. Jack seemed to mull over what she'd said. At first, she was pretty sure she saw dread in his face. Then he grinned and murmured, "Not if we break it off right now."

For a moment, she took him seriously — and his reply made her eyes sting. But when his smile made it clear what he really meant — he was agreeing that they'd become a couple — she was pleased. Not that she had intended that — either in what she'd just said or in inviting him to stay over. If anything, what she'd wanted from him was casual sex. But since they'd seen each other for months before they ended up in bed, there was no way it could have been casual. Even in the act itself, each had been overly careful, each a little too sensitive to the other. Neither could let go. So for Suzanne, that first sex hadn't been, as they called it, "fulfilling." But it had been sweeter than she'd imagined. And that was fine with her. That was better than fine.

At least she hadn't been a virgin. Before she graduated from Hollins, she'd had a relationship with a Washington and Lee boy who was so pretty, she expected him to drop her. He did, but not soon enough. He'd taken Suzanne's giving him her virginity as a sign that she loved him more passionately than the other girls he'd slept with. She'd given it because she wanted to be rid of it, but her gift had turned the boy sentimental, and he was reluctant to let her go. She'd had to make him look like a fool in front of his fraternity brothers a couple of times before he stopped calling and inviting her up to Lexington.

As she got to know Jack, however, she suspected something mysteriously good in him. It tantalized her that she couldn't name it. He was certainly considerate, but that wasn't it. He was also nice-looking, though not what she'd call handsome — his features were too asymmetrical to turn anybody's head. But he was taller and thinner than he'd first seemed, which Suzanne appreciated when she got a look at him without his clothes on. He wasn't muscular, but he had wide shoulders, thin hips, and not much fat around his waist. And though his wardrobe was dull as pigeon feathers, he dressed carefully. Now, remembering those clothes, Suzanne understood the ambivalence he must have felt about them. Even though he'd got a job as a junior reporter for the *Post,* the clothes he wore would have been right for a young banker or State Department official. Jack said the *Post* was assigning him stories for its financial pages, which was at least half true. But those suits and shirts and ties and shoes, she later learned, had been bought for him by his mother and father, who, if they'd had their way, would have seen their son with an office at Chemical Bank.

As it turned out, Jack invited Suzanne to meet his family before she asked him to meet hers. They flew up from National to La Guardia, took a cab to Manhattan, entered a building at Park Avenue and East Seventy-second Street, and stepped into an elevator that required less than half a minute to bring them to the nineteenth floor. It was about four-thirty, and they'd left Washington around two. Suzanne felt as if she'd arrived before she was ready. A maid welcomed them, told them she'd take care of their luggage, and directed them to the living room. "I'm sorry," Jack murmured in the corridor.

"For what?" she whispered. She was distracted by the individually lighted paintings on the walls of the front hall. She knew what she was seeing — there were a couple of early

Wyeths and a Rockwell Kent and a Jack Wesley. They raised her already high level of anxiety.

"They're rude," he said in so low a voice she could barely hear him. Then, from a door on the other side of the living room, Jack's mother, in a grand rustling of fabric, was walking toward them, smiling, her hands extended, as if for photographers. Suzanne imagined herself running, frantically pushing the elevator button.

"Jack, dear," Mrs. Nelson said, pecking his cheek and patting his arm before she pivoted.

"Suzanne," she said, grasping both of Suzanne's hands and pulling back to look at her. That smile really was a killer. "Jack's told me all about you," Mrs. Nelson said.

What could he tell you? He doesn't know a freaking thing. For a moment Suzanne thought she'd said the words aloud. Images from her childhood in Stevens Creek swept through her mind — including the path at her grandparents' place, through the weedy grape arbor, down the hill to the outhouse. She even got a whiff of the fecal air inside that closet-sized shack. Then she heard herself saying words that felt and tasted both odious and inevitable on her tongue: "Yes, Jack has told me so much about you, too."

Remembering the three of them standing in the sunlit living room, Suzanne focused on a split-second exchange between Jack and herself. Jack's face told her, *So now you see how it is. I can't tell you how ashamed I am of all this and how, in spite of how much I despise it, I can't break away.* And she intended her return look to convey, *Yes, I do see how it is. Your mother scares the hell out of me, and so does this apartment. But please don't look to me for help. I'm a coward, too.*

Shortly after, Jack's father — as tanned as if it had been August rather than April — joined them for cocktails. The four of them discussed galleries and artists and the prices and values of paintings. Suzanne understood that the Nelsons had chosen the topic to honor the graduate work she was doing in art history; the conversation, however, grated on her nerves and went on so long, she thought she would faint before they finally took a cab to a restaurant on Fifty-third Street. Just as they were being seated, Mr. Nelson leaned across the table, winked, and said, "Suzanne, you and I know most paintings are a waste of good canvas — or paper or whatever. A picture is worthless unless someone wants it. How valuable it is depends on what a person is willing to pay for it. Isn't that right?"

She smiled politely and paused before she spoke. "Well, sir, what if I want a picture but don't have any money? Or it's too big for my house?"

"Still worthless," he said, smiling and shaking his head. "Worthless until I write the check." And he tapped the table with his index finger.

Until that moment, Suzanne thought he was joking. Then she wasn't sure. It disturbed her that she couldn't tell whether the man was saying something so subtle that she wasn't getting it or whether he was asserting his status as a person wealthy enough to buy paintings. She thought he probably meant to be sociable, but he made her uncomfortable, so at dinner, she willed herself into drinking too much wine. She wanted to behave disgracefully, but she couldn't manage it. In fact, as the evening wore on — and she really did put away more wine than she'd ever drunk at any one time — she felt increasingly sober. By the time they were back in the apartment and she'd made her excuses to go to bed, she felt violated by the afternoon and evening. She'd been crushed by the conversation and manners of Jack's parents, though of course she had been a willing participant, a collaborator, a consenting adult. And how she felt about Mr. and Mrs. Nelson was exacerbated by her certainty that they had done their best to be hospitable. They had even shown her that they liked her. *And I thought my parents were grotesque* was the sentence that amused her enough to fall asleep.

The next morning, when she was reading in bed, there was a soft knock at the guest room door and a voice saying, "It's me." It was nearly nine o'clock. She put on her robe — she'd bought both it and her nightgown for this occasion — and unlatched the door, and there stood Jack, holding a tray with a silver coffee pot, creamer, and sugar bowl, along with china cups and saucers for both of them. He wasn't smiling — his expression was a little grim. Neither of them spoke as he stepped into the room, set down the tray, and turned toward her. His face made Suzanne shiver. Had anyone ever looked at her *that* nakedly? *He thinks he's weak:* she understood him as certainly as if he'd handed her a written note. And she quickly understood something else: *He doesn't mind if I know it.*

Suzanne was twenty-six years old. She was about to finish her dissertation on Caravaggio, which her adviser at Johns Hopkins deemed publishable. The same adviser assured her that after the visual arts interviews were held in New York in January, she would be offered a tenure-track position at a good university. And she was beginning to accept her professors' opinion that she was an accomplished person, one who could carry out scholarly research of lasting importance. To herself, she was willing to admit that she probably was exceptional. She didn't dwell on the point, but given her belligerently unexceptional family and the anticultural values of the place in the world where she'd grown up, Stevens Creek, Virginia, she was, it might be said, a phenomenon. She couldn't explain how she had become who she was. Most of the time, her life seemed to her a chain of accidents and coincidences that could as easily have led her to be an assistant manager at the Kroger's in Galax, like her sister Bonnie. Suzanne was as surprised as anyone that things had turned out for her as they had. But she also knew that she'd made choices and had worked long, long hours and that nobody would know how hard she'd tried.

He thinks he's not strong enough to get free. He's just as bad off as I am. The revelation felt like a violent push backward by a huge bully. Suzanne caught a glimpse of the relentless struggle of his life. *And mine, too. The two of us. Every waking hour given to escaping who we are. My God, how hard we try!* All that effort came from her yearning to be free of her parents and her house and her sisters and her town and her school and her teachers and she didn't even know what else, maybe even the bars of her baby crib and the air she started breathing in the hospital where she was born. It was the same for Jack; she saw it in his face. For both of them, there would never be an end to this hateful struggle.

She started to move toward Jack, thinking she would embrace him and they would stand there and weep quietly together. But in the instant, she realized crying wasn't at all what she wanted. Instead of going to him, she quietly latched the door behind her. Then, leaning back to brace her shoulders and her hands against it, she met his eyes and whispered, "What do you think?"

She expected him to shake his head.

His expression changed. What had been grim despair became a devilish grin. "I think we can, I think we can," he whispered. He stepped out of his loafers and unbuttoned his shirt while she slipped off her robe. She offered a hand to help steady him while he took off his pants. Dropping her pajama bottoms, she was a trifle self-conscious, but it was only a moment until they were under the covers. From then on, everything went slowly. Snuggled in the guest room bed with Jack was the coziest experience Suzanne could remember. Her whole body thrummed with the excitement of what they were up to. They had to be quiet, but the necessity of silence, an element missing from their previous attempts, enhanced the act. Afterward, to herself, Suzanne would say, *It was very fulfilling.* Sometimes she would say — to herself, of course — *I came like a freight train. I came like the Fourth of July. I came like a sea elephant.* She had a Stevens Creek way to put it, too: *I came pretty goddamn good.*

"Please explain this to me again." The note of forced patience in Suzanne's voice touched off an alarm in Jack's brain. "We're having the Halvorson's Quartet over here on Sunday afternoon?"

"No, darling. We're not having them in the sense of *having* them. We're just letting them use our living room for their rehearsal. They need a place to rehearse this week, and I thought that since you and I are usually on the go on Sunday afternoons —"

"Jack, we're not on the go on Sunday afternoons. That's the one time of the week when we relax and spend a little time together — in the living room. You listen to your opera program, while I read the *Times* and work the crossword puzzle."

"Well, that's exactly what I mean, darling. Instead of listening to the opera, this Sunday we'll have live music for our time together. It'll be an elegant occasion." And even as the words whistled across his tongue, Jack knew it was a mistake to sound out "elegant" as he'd just done, so that it sounded — all too clearly to his ear — like "Elly-gant." He noted a slight tightening of Suzanne's lips. She had to know something was up.

Jack had always assumed he was like his father, a man who

didn't make a lot of mistakes, especially when it came to social matters. But the nearer they came to Sunday afternoon, the more clearly he saw that he had committed a blunder of high magnitude. Mac probably didn't want the Nelsons hanging around the quartet's rehearsal, and Jack had no desire to sit for several hours in the same room with his wife and his lover — and three other witnesses. He tried to prepare himself.

He listened to his recordings of the Guarneri String Quartet playing the late Beethoven quartets; these were CDs he'd had before he met Elly Jacobs. Listening to them now was disturbing. He owned a superior stereo system, but no matter how far up he turned the volume, the music remained distant. His mind wandered as he listened. Even when he concentrated, he felt nothing. He saw himself as the emotionally inadequate musical oaf he had always suspected he was — a thought that was perversely comforting. It was followed, however, by a notion that was truly distressing.

If Jack was all these selves — the oaf, the responsive noble soul, the husband of Suzanne, the lover of Elly, the successful businessman, the liar, the truth teller — then what was at the center? What held these personalities together? The answer went hand in hand with the question. Nothing. Nothing whatsoever. Mentally, he pulled the plug on himself. The soiled residue of Jack Nelson swirled and gurgled down the drain. He was nobody. He was a series of masks, a pretender even to himself, and behind the last mask was a void.

The upheaval stayed with him through the time approaching the rehearsal. He distracted himself by preparing for the Halvorson's; he'd been around them enough to know how the seats should be arranged. Saturday evening, just before Suzanne and he were to go out to dinner with a new client and his wife, Suzanne came downstairs, fastening an earring as she stepped into the living room. Jack was preoccupied. "Do you think they'll get enough light from the windows?" he asked. "Or should I move some lamps over here?"

Standing beside him, Suzanne considered his arrangement of the four chairs. She was still for such a length of time that Jack sneaked a glance at her and only then noticed her new black dress and bright flowered scarf. She looked so stunning, he was embarrassed not to have said something, not to have complimented her on how the dress set off her figure. That might have put the moment right. Now, it was too late; he couldn't admit that when she first came downstairs she was nearly invisible to him. So the two of them continued to stare at the four empty chairs. Finally, to grant them license to leave the room, Jack murmured, "I think it's okay."

On Sunday mornings, Jack regularly played tennis with his men's doubles group at the club, while Suzanne, in her office at the Art Department, tried to catch up on her administrative duties. This Sunday, however, Jack canceled his lunch with Bill Roberts and Sandy Yondo, his accountant acquaintances who allowed him to pick their brains in exchange for eggs Benedict and champagne at Leunig's. He didn't expect Suzanne to cut short her working time; he preferred to fuss alone over the preparations for the rehearsal. He had even ordered a tray of hors d'oeuvres, which he picked up on his way home after tennis. His theory was that if his arrangements were exactly right, the afternoon would not become the disaster he feared, a vision of Suzanne and Elly screaming at each other, himself trying to calm them, and Mac Delgado, Caroline Wadhams, and Patty Magistrale politely observing their moment of disgrace. The hors d'oeuvres — along with the seating arrangement, the angle of light from the windows, and the 206 other details to which he had so painstakingly attended — would prevent such a scene.

Mac and Patty were the first to arrive, Mac in his usual tight black pants and loose-fitting white shirt. "Really decent of you, man," he said, offering his hand. When Jack shook it, the hand was a dead fish; nevertheless, he appreciated the gesture. This was the first time Mac had acknowledged him as anything more than a sometime customer of his place of employment. Jack was also amused to note that Mac's voice hardly conveyed any cultivation. If you went by his inflections, you'd figure Mac to be a heavy-equipment operator.

Patty gave him an absent-minded smile. She was carrying both her instrument and Mac's, which surprised Jack. He suspected Mac of having staged this small demonstration of Patty's devotion to him. She was wearing patched bluejeans and an old turtleneck — as if she thought the occasion was for picking apples rather than rehearsing a Beethoven quartet. She kept glancing at Jack, in an effort, he supposed, to remember who he was. And when she stepped into the foyer, she tripped over the edge of the carpet. "Sorry," she murmured as Jack caught her arm. Mac slicked back his hair and pretended not to notice.

While Mac and Patty moved to the living room, Caroline arrived on the front porch, and Jack stepped out to meet her. The October air was cool, still, and sweet; it made him yearn to spend the afternoon outdoors instead of being cooped up inside with the musicians, who probably wished him elsewhere. Caroline's appearance was that of a small-town librarian, right down to her white socks and walking shoes. "So kind of you to do this," she said, switching her cello case to her left hand and extending her right. Caroline's handshake was much firmer than Mac's, and her step was light as she maneuvered her sizable instrument past Jack and into the foyer. The moment gave him a glimpse of how much effort she expended in fending off despair and making her life worthwhile. "May the spirit of Beethoven bless your home," she said — which was, in Jack's opinion, an odd thing to say.

To avoid revealing their intimacy, he and Elly had agreed that she'd be late, the last to arrive. They would mingle with the others rather than let the heat build between them, as it did when they concentrated on each other. But now Jack began to worry whether Elly would arrive before her delay became conspicuous.

Suzanne's absence wasn't yet a surprise. On Sundays she often lingered in the office, tending to administrative details, because she didn't like them to interfere with her teaching responsibilities. At the moment it didn't matter, because Mac had decided to rearrange the four chairs. "This is real nice, man," he said, "but I want 'em to be looking out the windows. Today we're thinking about old deaf Beethoven dying and not wanting to give up any little bit of light, man. Not wanting to let go. We're thinking death and gray skies and closing time." Mac chanted to himself while moving the chairs into a semicircle facing the front windows, as if this afternoon's rehearsal would be a performance for an audience gathered in the front yard.

Mac, Caroline, and Patty seated themselves, took out their instruments, and began warming up. That was when Elly and Suzanne arrived. Suzanne pulled into the driveway just as Elly climbed out of her car on the street. Jack, who'd been standing at the open front door, watching for them and listening to the comically unorganized sounds of the instruments, now saw that the two women were about to converge on the front porch. He backed away, and though he couldn't hear what they said to each other, he could observe their facial expressions. The forced politeness was obvious as they began to speak. But when Suzanne said something accompanied by a smile, Elly's face relaxed, and she listened and responded. She set down her instrument case; Suzanne set down her bag. Gestures began to accompany their sentences; their faces grew more animated. It occurred to Jack that perhaps they were better friends than he'd known.

When they stopped talking and entered the house, Elly quickly took her place with the quartet, and Suzanne went upstairs to her study. Jack busied himself in the kitchen, making sure the refreshments would be ready when the group finished rehearsing. Then the warm-up noises suddenly ceased, so he slipped into the living room. He and Suzanne reached the sofa at the same time and plopped down beside each other like man-and-wife puppets. Jack was both embarrassed and amused.

Mac was instructing the group to play through each movement, to get a feeling for the entire composition, before they worked on the trouble spots. Then he talked quietly about Beethoven's life during the months the man had composed the last of his quartets. Unlikely phrases like "resignation informed by exaltation" and "rhythmic enlivening" found their way to Mac's tongue. Caroline observed him with rapt mindfulness. Patty Magistrale was distracted, adjusting her bow, looking for something in her case beside her chair; she seemed determined not to give her attention to Mac.

At first Elly was also unsettled. She fidgeted in her chair, glanced out a window, rubbed her neck, tucked a lock of hair behind her ear. Jack knew he shouldn't be watching her too closely. She was flushed, maybe still excited from her conversation with Suzanne and her hurry to take her seat. Then she slipped off her cardigan, bowed her head, and sat perfectly still. Jack could see that she was forcing herself to be quiet and listen to Mac. He knew she didn't want to be like Patty, who had not yet settled down. He worried that he was taking a risk by watching Elly so closely while sitting beside Suzanne. But he couldn't stop. That worn, ivory-tinted cotton tank-top exposed Elly's shoulders; the light from the window shone on her light-brown hair, which she had put up in a braid. Her slender neck, with her head bowed that way, was the most elegant human feature he'd seen; he was unable to look away.

Mac's voice became quieter and quieter, as if he meant to hypnotize the musicians. In nearly a whisper, he spoke of the privilege of playing the notes Beethoven had set down on paper a hundred and fifty years ago, and, with hardly a pause, he raised his violin to his shoulder and began softly counting the tempo for the opening movement. Apparently Mac's spell was properly cast, because Caroline, Elly, and even Patty were poised. The room suddenly resounded with deep chords, Elly bowed her violin with her arms and shoulders catching the window light, and Jack completely entered the dimension of pleasure.

Then he was hot. Or, rather, the side of him near Suzanne was hot. He'd lost track of time, but he knew that his gaze had been locked onto Elly for too long. Perhaps Suzanne had noticed, and the heat emanating from her was anger. He felt it from his knees to his face, as if her whole body were emitting furious energy. He didn't want to, but he made himself turn away from the quartet. Suzanne's eyes were not directed toward him; they were focused on the quartet. He couldn't tell exactly what she was looking at. Suzanne, her face flushed, glanced at him, shook her head, lifted her hand and waved it slightly, as if she were about to speak but had changed her mind. She cast her eyes down toward her lap, scooted closer to Jack, and rested her fingers on his sleeve. Her body was feverish enough to generate the fragrance of soap from her morning shower. And then Jack understood that she was stirred by the music. Relieved that his staring at Elly hadn't angered Suzanne, he closed his eyes and concentrated on the Beethoven.

Only between movements did Mac stop the group. At each pause, he spoke softly, not about the music itself, but about Beethoven and the circumstances of the composer's life. "What's important to remember is not that he almost committed suicide but that he chose not to," Mac told them. Jack thought it odd that Mac chose to talk of the composer rather than going over and over certain passages, as he ordinarily did in the rehearsals. Nevertheless, Jack had never heard such an inspiring performance by the Halvorson's. When the last chord of the final movement sounded, he opened his eyes, intending to look directly at Elly to signal his recognition of how beautifully the quartet had played. Instead, he saw Caroline Wadhams weeping openly, her face radiant from the window light. At first she looked toward Mac as if she were unaware of her tears. And though Jack couldn't read his expression, Mac steadily returned her look. When Caroline noticed Elly and Patty and Suzanne and Jack watching her cry, she touched her wet cheek and buried her face in her hands. "Don't look at me," she sobbed. "Please don't look at me."

Both Elly and Patty reached out toward the older woman. Even Suzanne — who knew Caroline only slightly — rose to go to her. Mac apparently didn't share Jack's embarrassment over Caroline's tears. He sat calmly, loosening his bow and setting it into the case; then he took out a cloth and began wiping his violin. Aware that Jack was still seated on the sofa, he asked, "Did you say there was something to eat?"

"Yes," Jack said. "Of course there is. Thanks for reminding me." He was grateful for a reason to leave the living room and the three younger women clustered around Caroline, patting her shoulders and assuring her that the music was so beautiful that they, too, felt like crying. Caroline explained that the entire day had set her on edge and made her vulnerable to the Beethoven, which she'd never played all the way through with the group. She was sure it would never happen again. What she didn't mention was what Jack suspected: that Mac's voice had affected her. As Jack carried in the tray of hors d'ouevres, he had a spiteful urge to say, "It was Mac's talking that made you cry, Ms. Wadhams! Why don't you admit it?" But an impulse saved him from making such a clumsy remark.

Suzanne and Elly were again drawn into an intense conversation. Caroline, having recovered herself, sought out Mac to discuss certain passages with him. Because he and Patty weren't engaged with the others, Jack felt obliged to stand beside her. They had no choice but to talk to each other.

Patty interrupted his polite remarks about how thrilled he was to hear the quartet in his own living room. "I have to tell you something, Mr. Nelson," she said. What from a distance had looked like a smile was now, up close, a grimace. "I hate that piece. I know Mac wants to play it, and I know he wants me not to screw up the viola part. All this week I worked by myself; I practiced for hours every day; and I can only barely get through the thing. I'm going to keep working on it, and I'm going to do the concert next week. But that's it. While we were playing that last movement, I figured it out. Playing in this group makes me miserable. It's screwing up my life. I'm going to tell Mac tonight. No more quartet for me after next Sunday. If Mac cares about me, he's going to have to let me quit."

Patty was probably telling him the news because she needed to put it into words to make it real. Her confiding in him wasn't a matter of trust; in fact, his being a near-stranger may have been what gave her the freedom to say it. Nevertheless, her statement made something crazy rise up in him: *he* could take

Patty's place in the Halvorson's. *He* could still read music — he knew that from having looked at the scores in Elly's apartment. He had even plinked on Elly's violin enough to know he remembered some of the fingering from his childhood training. He'd have to take leave from the office. He'd have to work on the instrument every waking hour. He'd have to take lessons every day, and the group would have to help him, but . . .

Even as these notions presented themselves, his sensible side pooh-poohed them, assessed them for what they were — the pipe dreams of a middle-aged man, a man afraid that he might amount to nothing. He congratulated himself on recovering his common sense before he'd said anything foolish to Patty. Indeed, he was about to ask her not to make a hasty decision about quitting the Halvorson's when Suzanne touched his shoulder.

"Jack, do you mind driving Elly home? She's got something in her eye."

He scanned Suzanne's face carefully. There was no smile lurking at the corners of her mouth; she seemed sincere, though Jack knew you could never be sure about another person, even your spouse. And Elly was, apparently, in trouble. When he looked in her direction, she stepped nearer and showed him a red, teary eye. Having closely searched Suzanne's face and now Elly's, Jack felt disoriented. He went out to the porch while Elly gathered her things and said her goodbyes. On the street, she handed him her car keys, but neither of them said a word. A warm, light rain was falling, but across the lake there was sunlight. The damp air cleared Jack's head, and he heard himself whistling something vaguely like a Beethoven melody as he slid behind Elly's steering wheel.

While Jack drove away from his house, he felt a pleasant tension. Elly stashed her handkerchief in her purse, leaned back in her seat, and rested her left hand on his thigh, high up. Whatever had been in her eye seemed to have gone away. "Drive fast," she said softly. "Take some chances, Jack. I'll make it worth your while."

At Elly's apartment door, there was no question as to whether he was going to come in. Once inside, Elly turned, her arms lifted toward his shoulders, and they were kissing greedily before he'd locked the front door behind them. The rain had left a mist on her face that made her skin slick against his. "That whole thing made me so hot," Elly murmured.

"What whole thing?" he murmured back. They were grappling at each other's clothes and backing their way through Elly's living room toward the bedroom.

"You saw Caroline crying? Well, that's how it affected her. This is what it did to me." Elly was pushing down her panty hose and laughing.

"The Beethoven?"

Naked now, Elly leaped sideways onto her bed, still laughing. "The Beethoven, Mac's sexy voice, talking with your uptight wife, then you and your uptight wife in your American Gothic pose on the sofa, the window light, this crazy weather . . . What's taking you so long, Jack? If you don't get in this bed pretty quick, you're going to miss your chance."

So he got on the bed as Elly had, by leaping sideways like a porpoise. And she wasn't exaggerating about how turned on she was. Jack was astonished — even a bit intimidated — by the powerful force moving her. But he could tell that it had nothing to do with him. An acquaintance had once disparaged a businesswoman they knew by saying, "She's so horny, she'd fuck a doorknob." That was the crudest thing Jack had heard anyone say about a woman, and the phrase — and the image — stuck in his mind. This afternoon, after they'd been in bed only a little while, he wondered whether he was Elly's doorknob.

So he looked for a graceful excuse to leave. "Since I have to walk home," he announced at an appropriate stopping place, "I'd better get going."

Elly sat up, holding the bedcovers to her chest. She looked hard at his face, then down at his chest — which admittedly was not much of a chest. Jack wasn't a hairy fellow; he'd never tried to tan that part of his body, and his only exercise was the occasional tennis match. Elly knew exactly where to direct her eyes to remind him of his most vulnerable physical feature. Then she swung her legs over the side of the bed and stood up, still holding the bedcovers to herself and ripping them off the bed as she moved away. He lay on the bottom sheet, exposed as a fishing worm. "You don't have to go, Jack," Elly said with her back to him. "The fact is, you were never here in the first place."

While he put on his clothes, she gazed out the bedroom window. The funny thing was, she kept the bedcovers clutched to her front, but her back, from her shoulders to her feet, was uncovered and right out there for him to see. He didn't know whether Elly gave it any thought, though it was hard to imagine that she didn't. It was quite a pretty back, and as fetching a backside as Jack had ever seen. Figuring this was the last time he'd see it, he felt remorseful.

"My best to your wife," Elly murmured as he left the room. She never turned away from the window.

La Tour's home comes into view as Vivienne reaches the top of the hill at the far side of Lunéville. Though the property sits alongside a village street, it has the appearance of a prosperous farmhouse. A low wall surrounds the grounds; the outbuildings and additions are attached to the main house. This afternoon, in the sunlight, the house generates a sleepy atmosphere, as if every living creature has settled down for a nap. Perspiring and a little out of breath, Vivienne stands and studies the place that is so familiar to her. Always, in the past, she encountered servants and chickens and goats and dogs. Today there's no movement; there are no sounds.

She considers turning around and walking back home. Nothing requires her to make this visit. She doesn't need the picture — she doesn't know what she'd do with it if the old painter does agree that it belongs to her. She'd have to hide it from her parents. Anyway, La Tour may be ill, unable to speak to her. But even if he's well, there's little reason for her to hope he can help her with her lying ways. He knows all the stories she told him about herself, but he himself is probably a grand liar — though she can think of no particular lie she ever caught him at. She doesn't, however, want to pursue this errand any further. Seeing the house asleep at the top of the hill is perhaps all she needs to cast the disturbance from her mind. After all, her lying is a problem only to herself; neither her mother nor her father has yet confronted her with one of her fabrications. And maybe now her story of La Tour and the picture can take its proper place in the distant past. Vivienne sighs with relief. She has taken a step back toward the village when she hears a muffled yip.

At the gate, low to the ground, is a demon face.

"Caravaggio!" The dog she remembers as La Tour's favorite lies, belly down, at the gate, its grotesque head resting on its extended paws. It barked at Vivienne, though in such a feeble voice that it may as well have been a cat meowing. Vivienne steps briskly to the gate and bends to greet Caravaggio.

"You little hell-dog, you recognized your Vivienne, didn't you?" She speaks to the creature at some length before she touches it. When she does, she can feel a small death-dog residing within Caravaggio's torso, almost the size of the animal itself. Death is gradually swelling up inside Caravaggio. She feels it moving ever so slightly in the little body. She shivers and stands, ready to run down the hill. Instead, she clenches her teeth, scoops the dog into her arms — though she knows it never liked being picked up — and takes the path that leads around the house to the grape arbor, the shady place where La Tour's dogs like to spend their afternoons. "You can't lie out here in the hot sun, little hell-dog. You need to be with your brothers and sisters. You need some water," she croons. It doesn't struggle, but her hands discern various lumps just beneath the surface of Caravaggio's skin. Vivienne wonders whether it might die at this moment, just as she is carrying it to a cool place.

Suddenly, there's La Tour. Of course she nearly drops the dog, she's so startled. She's behind the old painter, who is leaning back in the huge chair from his library. The servants must have set it up here in the garden, with cushions under every part of his body. She can hear his slow, deep breathing. He hasn't seen her; his eyes are closed, and he may be napping. She notices, too, that around the edges of the garden, in the shade of bushes and shrubs, his other dogs are lying, too torpid in the heat to rouse themselves to bark at her. Breathing softly, with Caravaggio clutched to her chest, Vivienne gazes at the tufts of white hair that spring from La Tour's head. She doesn't remember ever seeing him without one of his wigs. At the moment he looks so ancient that he must be beyond death.

"Please, my dear." His voice rumbles out of him, the words muffled, because he's speaking to her while he's waking up. And how does he know she's here? "Please step around in front of me. I haven't seen you in such a long time."

Vivienne's heartbeat quickens as she moves around his chair. This man has such power over her! If La Tour dies this afternoon, he may take her with him. He may ask her to follow him into death, and if he commands her, how could she refuse him?

La Tour's face is paler and smoother than she remembers it, as if in growing older — and he has aged so much that it seems more like ten years than two since she last saw him — he's returning to what he looked like as a baby. But his eyes have moved deeper into age while his face has retreated toward youth. The blue of his eyes is a milky gray; there will be only whiteness in another two years. He blinks as she moves to stand before him.

"You've brought my Caravaggio back to me, haven't you, my dear? Very kind of you. I had thought my old friend was deserting me this afternoon, though he usually keeps me company. Will you set him in my lap?"

Though she is loath to come closer to him, Vivienne does as La Tour asked. When she releases Caravaggio into the nest the old painter makes with his hands, her body cools immediately, as if she's broken a fever.

"There, yes, you little traitor." La Tour caresses Caravaggio and arranges the bug-eyed creature across his melon-shaped belly. A pregnant old man is what Vivienne thinks as she looks at him. The silliness of the idea comforts her enough so that she no longer feels helpless as she stands before him. She can still mock him. But when he turns his sea-pale eyes to her again, the heat returns like an illness.

"So now, my dear Vivienne Lavalette, daughter of the shoemaker of Lunéville, human child marked with the sign of the wolf, you've come back after these years. You're kind to visit an old man."

Vivienne resists the impulse to reach across herself and touch her shoulder. She remains before him in the pose he taught her as appropriate for a well-bred young lady, one foot slightly before the other, hands crossed in front of her skirt, shoulders back, and chin held high. She hasn't consciously chosen to stand this way, but now she appreciates it. It lets her look down from a certain height at La Tour, which suits her mood. She's aware of the sun's warmth on her shoulders and of how the rose hedge to her right must set off her brown dress. "Sir, I came to talk with you about the painting — the one you did of me with the yellow cloth?"

La Tour waves his hand a little, by which she understands that the painting is in the studio behind him. Perhaps he also means that it has no value to him and that she may take it home with her. Or perhaps he's indicating that he knows which painting she's talking about. At any rate, she's encouraged by his gesture.

"The light out here is good for you, Vivienne Lavalette. Did you know that? I'd not be surprised if you did. You're a clever girl."

Vivienne can't help smiling. She remembers what it was like to be with La Tour — as if her presence, the mere sight of her, was a tonic to him. It was as if she were invisible to everyone but him. She asks, politely, "Do you still paint, sir?"

The old man laughs in such a stifled way that it sounds like weeping. His shoulders shake. Then he says, "Was I a painter? Was that what I was? I tell you, Vivienne Lavalette, I don't have painting in my mind. I have pictures — pictures in my studio, pictures that I know people paid me for and took away and I haven't seen since. But it's the pictures I remember, not the painting. I know I must have done it. The one you're talking about, the one with the yellow drapery and the dark background and your skin that I worked hard to make a color for — I can feel that picture with my body. But painting it? I can't have done that. I was too old. I couldn't stand up long enough to put more than three brushstrokes to a canvas."

"You painted it, sir. I watched you do it. Every day for many days, in your studio. I talked to you, and you stood at your easel and painted while I held the yellow drapery."

There is a long moment of quiet. Vivienne's skin prickles.

"You want that picture, don't you, Vivienne Lavalette?" La Tour's voice is an insinuating whisper.

A sweat breaks out across her forehead. "Yes, sir."

"Have you asked yourself why you want it?"

"No, sir."

"Do so. Ask yourself right now."

The silence folds around them; the world drops away except for the bright greenness of La Tour's garden. A bird trills in a nearby tree. Vivienne hears the hum of bees in the flowerbed.

"Why do you want it?"

"Because I love it, sir."

Although she'd not thought about it, she knows to say these words. And no sooner are they out of her mouth than La Tour's head snaps down in a nod. She's given the right answer, yet panic rises in her. What if that's a lie? Isn't she lying? Doesn't she want the painting because it will be payment for what La Tour stole when he painted her? And when he set the hair on her shoulder so that she had to know about it? That's what she wants to take away from him! She doesn't love the picture.

"I'm lying, sir," she murmurs.

"If you are lying, Vivienne Lavalette — and it is by no means certain that you are" — his voice is pitched exactly to hers — "it makes not the slightest difference."

So this is what he has to tell her about her lying. What a thought! It doesn't matter. But is that really so?

La Tour looks hard and long at her, then makes another gesture, this one a subtle beckoning with his crooked fingers toward the chair beside his in the shade of the huge chestnut tree.

Vivienne looks to see whether the servants are watching them from the house. They're not; she and the old painter have the garden to themselves. She well understands La Tour, and she sighs, because she knew this was coming — his request to see her naked. She had hoped the moment would transport her back to the child she was when she'd posed for him. Instead, now that he has asked, she feels as ancient as he is. Yes, I'm going to be an old whore, she tells herself, and undoes the buttons down the front of her brown dress. Then it's easy. She steps out of her sandals, and her clothes and undergarments fall away onto the grass as she steps slowly toward the chair. The warm air feels pleasant on her skin. She looks down at her body. I have excellent breasts, she reminds herself. He likes them. She twists her head to see the back of her shoulder, but, as always, it is just out of sight. She turns to the side so that La Tour can see that part of her, and she knows now what she didn't know then — that her shoulder fascinates him. She wants him to see it again.

She sits in the chair. She's not comfortable, but she tries to relax, as she did in the old days. Since he gives her no directions for posing, she tries to imagine herself in a picture he is painting, with sunlight and shadow rippling over her skin. She concentrates on the crimson roses in the bright sunlight across the grass. A dog in that part of the garden lifts its head, blinks at her, then returns to its nap. The world goes silent. Out here, under the tree, the quiet is so deep that she hears only her own slow breathing.

Suzanne had invited Jack to visit her home and meet her family, too. Though Jack had never urged her to take him to Stevens Creek, it seemed only fair. She wondered whether he really wanted to go, but then assumed that he did, because he'd taken her to meet his parents. Why would he have done that if he hadn't wanted to meet hers? At any rate, she was certain it was the right thing to do — the only thing to do if she wanted to continue to see Jack. Dreading it like surgery, she'd invited him, and he'd gravely accepted and offered to drive them down.

"You have a car?"

He nodded.

"You bought a car?"

"No, I've had this one since boarding school. I don't use it in the city. Most of the time I even forget I have it. It's in a garage a few blocks from my place."

"Jack!"

He grinned and shook his head as if to agree that he was a hopeless case. Suzanne did her best to rein in her feelings, but in fact she was outraged that in the entire ten months she'd known the man, he hadn't mentioned owning a car. They still had separate apartments in D.C., but it seemed a violation of trust.

"It's just an old car. I mean, I guess it's an antique, but that's because I've had it so long. We don't have to take it if you don't want to."

When she asked him to show it to her, he was quick to agree. The next afternoon, a Sunday, they walked the five blocks to Jack's place on Nebraska Avenue, where he picked up the keys, and then the three blocks over to the garage on Fifty-first. It wasn't a regular parking garage; it was a long-term rental warehouse, and most of the cars were covered with tarps. When he pulled the cover off his, even in the dim light of the building, the thing sparkled. It was a Cadillac, a navy-blue 1963 El Dorado with white leather seats and a hood that seemed to Suzanne about a foot longer than any she'd seen. Standing in the presence of the Cadillac, she gradually understood what the deal was: Jack's parents had given it to him when he was at Choate, probably on the birthday when he was old enough to get his license. As he grew older, he also grew more ashamed of the thing. Now, while they stood beside the car, he shook his head as if it had made a foolish remark, and asked Suzanne, "Should we take it down there?"

When she recalled her pause before answering, she blushed! She'd known what it would mean to her mother and father — especially what it would mean to her sisters — if she rode into Stevens Creek in that Cadillac. She'd almost laughed aloud at the thought of Bonnie and Gail watching that slab of a car door swing open and seeing their little sister climb out. They'd pee in their pants, the two of them! "Jack" — she touched his arm and knew that her face was probably the most vivacious she'd shown him — "Jack, now that I've seen your car, I can't imagine going home any other way."

She began to figure out how long it was since she'd been home — about a year and a half, she thought. She'd kept in touch as she'd done during her last year at Hollins, calling her parents on Sunday afternoon every couple of weeks. She'd had to struggle to make those conversations last more than five minutes, and eventually her parents stopped asking when she'd be coming home. Somewhere during those college years, Suzanne got the idea that her parents didn't mind her not coming to visit.

She was reluctant to admit this to herself, but she may as well have, because whenever she did go, she remembered hating the years she'd spent in her childhood home. Again and again — grown woman though she was — she tried to demonstrate to her parents that she was a good daughter, maybe the best of all daughters. She kept hoping that if she explained her work at school, her goals, and the life she planned for the future — if she could make them truly understand her — they would suddenly realize what a treasure she was. But the results of her efforts were always the opposite of what she wanted. As she pursued her parents from room to room, their moods became darker, they had less to say, and they all too obviously avoided situations in which she might go on talking. Watching TV was their strategy. She couldn't believe the programs her parents watched — game shows, soap operas, stock car races, weather. Still, she couldn't banish her desire to please them. And she couldn't please them in their terms; she couldn't bear sitting through five minutes of "Jeopardy," their favorite. So it was by unspoken agreement that she stopped going home. When she entered the graduate program at Hopkins, she always had course work to do, and there were her part-time jobs and her teaching assistantships and, of course, her impossibly demanding, never-ending dissertation. She'd become used to not seeing her family, and her family seemed not to notice her absence.

Now she was bringing Jack Nelson to meet them.

It was June, a pretty time of the year to visit the Blue Ridge Mountains of Virginia, a pleasant time to travel down Interstate 81 in a smooth-riding, air-conditioned car. They stopped at Hollins, where Suzanne took Jack on a quick tour but found none of her old professors on campus. Even so, the graceful willows beside Tinker Creek where she and Jack walked hand in hand put her in a good mood. When they finally pulled into the driveway of the Yarborough homeplace — the two-story clapboard box that her father kept painted and well-maintained — she felt a gush of affection for her family. Her mother and father and her sisters were all sitting on the porch, dressed up for company, with a pitcher of lemonade, a tray of glasses, and a plate of cookies ready to be served. Maybe because she was looking at them from the passenger seat of Jack's Cadillac — and maybe, too, because she'd made the trip to New York and met his family — at that moment, Suzanne felt proud of these people who'd had so much to do with who she was. Her mother and her sisters were wearing make-up and their pretty summer dresses. Even though this was a Saturday, a day he ordinarily spent in work clothes, mowing the grass and puttering around the yard, her father was wearing a white shirt and a tie. Maybe she couldn't make her parents understand her, but she could stop being judgmental about them. And her sisters had the right to live in whatever way they wanted. Were these not hard-working and decent and responsible people? And by presenting themselves this way to the young man she had brought to meet them, were they not demonstrating their care for her?

Suzanne opened the door of the air-conditioned car and stood up in the sunlight. The heat of the afternoon and the smell of the air around her parents' house gave her the sensation of having stepped back through time to her childhood. "Hello, Mama," she called, stretching on tiptoe and reaching up her arms. "Hello, Papa," she called. It amused her that Jack had never heard her refer to her parents this way. But he may as well get used to the idea that she was a Stevens Creek girl — she herself had been trying almost her entire life to get used to it. With Jack following her, she moved to the porch, and, as if they'd rehearsed it, her parents and sisters gave her long hugs. Maybe to extract some love from her family, this was how she had to do it — stay away from them for three or four years and then ride home in a Cadillac.

While she performed the introductions, Suzanne couldn't help studying the face of each family member. Had she ever before looked at them so carefully? It was more than a little disturbing, because in the intensity of Suzanne's attention they were like actors, stiffly playing the roles of Bonnie and Gail and mother and father. Suzanne shook her head to clear it; she knew that the strangeness of coming home after being away so long was affecting her perceptions.

"Jack, our little Suzie didn't warn us you'd be so good-looking. We're going to have to hide you in the house, or every girl in Carroll County will be over here, trying to strike up a conversation with you."

Jack bashfully cast his eyes down. And did her mother actually wink at him? Not only had Suzanne never heard herself referred to as "little Suzie," but she'd never witnessed her mother being flirtatious. Flirtatiousness was just about the last trait she thought her mother possessed. Unfortunately, it made her appear ridiculous. It wasn't that Mrs. Nelson was unattractive; she'd kept herself thin, had an understated sense of style in her clothes, and a tasteful restraint in how she used make-up and cut her hair. Suzanne had theorized that her own "eye" for the visual arts must have come from her mother. The woman's charm — as far as Suzanne was aware of it — certainly wasn't in making flattering remarks to men half her age. She did recall that her mother's face would become animated on the rare occasions when she reminisced about growing up on a farm outside Hillsville. During those moments of nostalgia, energy rose in her and made her more attractive. But the simpering smile Suzanne saw now, as her mother engaged Jack in small talk, must be something she'd taken from TV. Suzanne assumed that Jack was both amused and embarrassed.

Her father cleared his throat. "That's a very handsome car you're driving, Jack. A 'sixty-five, isn't it?"

Jack turned his attention to her father. To Suzanne, the two men could have been chimpanzees in a laboratory experiment. Each one's face took on a companionable expression; each widened his eyes. There was a pause during which each seemed to be weighing the other's strengths and weaknesses.

"That's pretty close, sir. It's actually a 'sixty-three, but there were three or four years there when they didn't change the car much because it was selling well. Would you like to take her for a spin, sir?"

Take her for a spin? Now there was a phrase she'd never heard Jack Nelson use. But he had it right; it was exactly the language that would appeal to her father. And she saw from her father's face that he liked Jack's offering him the keys.

"Oh, no, I wouldn't want to get behind the wheel; I'd probably get excited and run it right up the side of a tree. But if you'll do the driving, I wouldn't mind taking a ride with you. Never been in a Cadillac."

"Richard, Jack is probably tired of driving. He's been on the road all day, you know."

"Oh, no, I'm not tired at all. I hate to admit it, but driving this car is just about my favorite form of recreation. I'd love to take you all for a ride, if you're up for it." Jack quickly stepped over to the car and began setting things from the back seat onto the grass at the edge of the driveway.

The upshot was — and it mildly astonished Suzanne to see how they negotiated it without her saying a word — that Jack took the four of them for a ride in the Cadillac. As they eased out of the driveway, with her father sitting sternly in the front while her mother and sisters giggled like teenagers in the back, it was nakedly evident to Suzanne that her parents and sisters wanted to be seen in that car by the citizens of Stevens Creek. She was pretty sure Jack had also understood what they wanted and was pleased to oblige.

They'd be gone at least an hour, more than that if they drove all the way to Galax. Suzanne might have been furious at being left behind, except, as it happened, this was exactly what she wanted — a little solitude in the old homeplace. Smiling, she slipped off her shoes and slowly walked around the yard, savoring the rough-and-smooth caress of the grass on her bare feet. She circled the house before she slipped through the screen door into the pantry and into the kitchen. There, she stood still, greedily sniffing the yeasty air.

Pink chicken parts had been dredged with flour, salt, and pepper; they lay neatly stacked on the cutting board beside the sink. Potatoes had been peeled, quartered, put in their pot, and covered with water. Green beans had been snapped and placed in their pot of water. Kneaded biscuit dough lay waiting in a pan covered with waxed paper. The bottle of Crisco stood beside the big black skillet on the stove. A salad had been prepared except for the tomatoes, which sat beside the bowl, ready to be cut and added just before being placed on the dining room table. If her mother had been challenged at the Pearly Gates and told that she must prepare a meal to determine whether she went to heaven or hell, her hope for salvation would have been this fried chicken dinner.

Suzanne imagined the six of them sitting down to the dinner around twilight. She could see her mother's eyes slyly studying Jack as he began to eat. Of course her mother would be watching to see whether he used his knife and fork to cut the chicken. If he used his fingers, her mother would have to watch even more carefully to see whether he did it naturally or was doing it to be sociable with his girlfriend's country family. And of course the entire family would be covertly paying attention to Suzanne as well. Would she have gone so far beyond her raising that she used a knife and fork? Nothing would be said about these choices, whatever they were. Suzanne could imagine another family dinner where there would be teasing or witty conversation about how an individual chose to eat his or her fried chicken. But *her* family would be making its silent judgments — its classically petty-minded Yarborough judgments. And when they got the chance to discuss among themselves Jack's and Suzanne's table manners, they would take pleasure in sharing their evaluations of the prodigal daughter and her fancy boyfriend.

She shuddered and walked quickly through the dining room

and living room, out to the cool hallway. Moving through the house hardly disturbed her concentration; she seemed to be gliding up the stairs and down the shadowy hall. She couldn't have named it, but she felt *this* was where she had needed to go — exactly here. Flowered curtains filtered the light; the air smelled of newly washed sheets and pillowcases, but the old smells were here, too, the paint on the walls, the varnish on the floor, the faint cedary fragrance from the drawers of her bureau. She watched a dust mote hanging in a shaft of light from the window. So quiet was the house, it could have been floating through outer space.

Now the child who'd so often retreated to this room carefully pulled out her small chair and sat down. This was where she would never be disturbed by anyone. When she'd started first grade, her father had bought students' desks at Sears, one for each daughter, and he'd borrowed Uncle Danny's pickup truck to haul them home. He was so proud of what he'd done that the rule of the Yarborough household became that if a girl was sitting at her desk, she was not to be bothered for any reason short of the house's being on fire. Suzanne's desk had been cleared of any trace of the past, but it faced the same window overlooking the same open field with a range of mountains in the distance, two shades of blue deeper than the sky. While sunlight baked the grassy field outside, her room was as cool and shadowy as a forest. Her pulse quickened: there she was, sitting on a rock beside an old dirt road, her hair thicker and darker than one expected of someone with such fair skin. Her arms, bare to the sun, would be burned if she didn't soon find a shady place. She tossed the mane of shiny black hair and turned a defiant face toward Suzanne.

Two beeps from Jack's Cadillac rolling into the driveway brought Suzanne out of her reverie. And when she stood up from the desk, she felt refreshed. Nevertheless, she dawdled, savoring the quiet of the room before she went downstairs to meet the noisy bunch as they trooped into the house.

Outside, the rain shower had passed, leaving the air clear and clean. Jack stood for a moment on the sidewalk outside Elly's apartment building, breathing that rich stuff into his body. Was she looking down on him from her bedroom window? No matter; it was exhilarating to have escaped. His life had been returned to him. When he started walking home, he felt uncommonly alive. To be outdoors on a late October afternoon — to be a living creature! — struck him as a privilege. Tawny light magnified each shape and shadow. Like bright paint, wet maple and butternut leaves coated the sidewalk and the street. The leaves adorned car roofs and hoods and sifted down through the air. College students he passed on the street had the faces of saints and angels. He wanted to touch their shoulders and tell them, *You look like Saint Francis. Do you know that? You're a remarkable creature!*

At the corner of Maple and Willard, he stopped, drinking in the view of the lake and the far mountains. He was still for such a length of time that a young man asked, "Are you okay, mister?" Jack waved and proceeded at his leisurely pace, absorbing all the sights. When he turned the corner and saw his own house, he felt a rush of emotion. Who was he to deserve such a home? What had he done to merit this life, which he had taken for granted until this very moment? What right did he have to breathe air so pure that it made him giddy?

He moved slowly up the driveway, past Suzanne's car and his. The back yard, with its own pattern of leaves on the wet grass, was streaked with sunlight and shadow. Reluctant to leave the outdoors, he stepped softly onto the porch and opened the back door with unusual quietness. Indoors, it was muggy, as if the rain had forced warmth into the house.

Suzanne was sitting in the living room. As if someone had placed a restraining hand against his chest, Jack stopped at the door. She was nude. With her head leaning back in her wing-back chair, her eyes closed, and her arms resting at her sides, she was shockingly pale. He stood ten feet away, expecting her to sense his presence, cover herself with her hands, leap from the chair, and dash toward the steps in the front hallway. Her legs, somewhat spread, extended before her, the knees bent. Her breasts stared at him. After several moments, when she didn't stir, he realized she was asleep. If he wished, he could walk over and examine her from different angles. Maybe one of Suzanne's artist friends had, as a joke, constructed a model of her, like one of those museum pieces that look like living people. But he could see her rib cage and belly moving slightly as she breathed. This was his living — albeit sleeping — wife, all right. He relaxed, eased himself into the room, and sat down on the sofa, facing Suzanne. He watched her as if she were television.

Marriage is a lot more peculiar than anyone imagines. That's what Jack decided as he calmly assembled a rational story of how Suzanne ended up in this chair without any clothes on.

When Mac and Patty and Caroline had packed their instruments and left the house, Suzanne had felt relief. Jack knew she loved the moment of closing the door behind guests. In the past, she'd broken into ridiculous songs about the people they'd just finished entertaining. So this afternoon, glad to be rid of the Halvorson's group, she planned to go upstairs and change into her lazy-evening-at-home clothes — that is, her slacks and her sneakers. On the four chairs where the musicians had sat were Suzanne's sweater, skirt, blouse, slip, bra, and — curled into a cat-sized wad of fabric — her underpants and panty hose. Because it was unseasonably warm in the house, she did a little strip there in the rehearsal space, keeping an eye on the windows to make certain no one saw her. She let her clothes fall on the chairs, humming as she undressed: Sweater for you, Patty; blouse for you, Caroline; to you, Elly, I give my skirt; and, oh, Mac, what about this slip? In her silly mood, she enjoyed the idea of being alone downstairs without her clothes. She strolled around the living room, trying out the air on her skin. The cover of the *Smithsonian* on the coffee table caught her eye, and she picked it up and sat down in the wing chair. While she leafed through the pages, a tremendous tiredness overcame her. It had always been easy for her to drop off to sleep, so she leaned back, let her eyes close . . .

All this Jack fathomed up with perfect clarity, because he knew his wife so well. And yet — this was what shocked him — he had never once sat and looked at Suzanne naked like this. Had he ever asked to do such a thing, she would have blushed. Had she ever asked whether she could sit and stare at him without his clothes on, he would have refused. For married people to do such a thing was, now that he considered it, warped. But there he was, taking a good long look at his wife.

Suzanne was tall and thin, but in the chair, her shoulders were slumped and her stomach pooched out. Her breasts, though small, had relaxed into middle age, he noticed. Her nipples were not erect; apparently they could not have cared less whether he stared at them. And he guessed it was several days since Suzanne had shaved her legs. Dark sprouts of hairs speckled her calves and thighs. He felt safe in assuming that had Suzanne expected him to see her naked, she'd have presented herself more favorably. Which may be what made the circumstance absorbing, seeing her in a way that she would never have permitted.

Jack focused so long and intently on his sleeping, naked wife that he began to hear soft phrases of the last movement of the Beethoven quartet — fragments of sound lingering in the room. He closed his eyes and listened.

Something, he sensed, had changed. Suzanne had opened her eyes and was regarding him. She hadn't moved, and she appeared calm. Modesty should have caused her to cover herself, but she seemed unaware of her nakedness.

"Mac told me —" she began. Then something caught in her throat, preventing her from going on.

Panic lifted Jack from the sofa and moved him toward her. "It's all over," he nearly shouted. "And there wasn't anything to it in the first place. She's nothing! Compared with you, she's less than nothing, my darling. I'm sorry I ever got involved with her. I know I'm a pig. I'm a classic pig! I know I don't deserve you, but I swear I'll do better. I've learned my lesson." He knelt by Suzanne's chair, clasping its arms, because he didn't dare touch her bare skin.

Her eyes widened. "I was going to say," she said, enunciating each word carefully, "that Mac told me he doesn't want to perform the Beethoven after all."

"What?"

"Mac said the quartet will never play the Beethoven better than they played it this afternoon. He said that when they let go of the last chord, he looked at Caroline's face and knew he would never play that piece again."

Jack searched for something to say. "I didn't know you even knew Mac," he murmured.

"I don't. His girlfriend had to go to work, so he stayed to help me clean up. He said he needed to do something to unwind; he was glad to have me to talk to."

Jack was quiet. If it was possible for a person to feel his life changing in a single moment, that was what he felt. His head bowed of its own accord. He let his forehead rest on his right hand, still holding the arm of the chair. After a moment he felt Suzanne's hand lightly touch the crown of his head, the place where his hair was starting to go.

"I wish you hadn't told me what you told me," she whispered.

"I do, too," Jack said.

Seconds ticked away.

"Well, maybe I don't wish it after all," she said.

"I guess I don't either," he replied.

Suzanne moved her hand from his head and stirred in her chair. "I should put some clothes on."

He gazed at her as she rose and couldn't help lifting his eyebrows.

"I don't know," she said. "While Mac was here, there was a lot of energy in the house. He was so stirred up by the music that he kept talking and walking around. And when he left, it was as if a storm had ended. There wasn't a sound, and I went to the window and saw that soft rain falling. The only sensible thing to do was take off my clothes and sit down with the *Smithsonian*."

She paused, and then she, the least giggly woman Jack knew, giggled. "What can I say?" She shrugged. "I've been under a lot of stress lately." She smiled at him, kneeling beside her chair. He shrugged in return, and she headed up the stairs.

"Elly Jacobs is total bitch," she called to him from halfway up.

"Yes," Jack said. Even as he pronounced the word, a voice inside him whispered, *No, she isn't.* He continued kneeling by the empty chair and heard Suzanne's footsteps move down the hallway toward their bedroom, then come back to the head of the staircase.

He could almost feel her trying to determine what she needed to say to him.

Jack waited. All was quiet. Suzanne was up there, naked in the hallway, and he was downstairs, kneeling by the chair. He held his breath, waiting for her to speak.

"If you even look at her again, I'll kick you out of the house, Jack," she said as matter-of-factly as if she were asking him to pick up something at the grocery store.

"All right." She said nothing more and didn't move, so the worst was over. "Thank you, darling," Jack called up to her. Suzanne didn't reply, but he heard her footsteps move down the hall again. Feeling released, he stood up and stretched.

Not looking at Elly Jacobs turned out to be no problem for Jack. She left Burlington at the end of the fall semester, having won a year's fellowship at the American Academy in Rome. And, as it turned out, that afternoon's rehearsal in the Nelsons' living room was the last time the members of the Halvorson's Quartet played together. Patty Magistrale informed Mac that she was quitting. On Monday, when Elly received the news of her fellowship, she immediately phoned Mac to tell him she was through playing with the group. So Mac canceled the Friends Concert. And when he walked over to Caroline's house to tell her what had happened — dreading how the bad news would affect her — Caroline confessed that she was relieved. Playing the Beethoven that afternoon had answered some questions she had been asking herself for years. Standing out on the front porch of the old Wadhams house, she told Mac that the rehearsal had given her what she needed to carry on the rest of her life. Mac didn't understand what she meant, but he said he felt pretty much the same. They gave each other a clumsy goodbye hug out there on the porch, though of course they continued to see each other every Thursday at noon when Caroline and her sister came for lunch at the restaurant where Mac worked.

How did Jack learn these details? His wife told him. At about the time she gave up the department chairmanship, she and Mac became good friends. The hour or so they'd spent together cleaning up the house after the rehearsal turned out to be a "bonding experience." Suzanne explained to Jack, "It's not romantic or sexual. He has Patty for that." Jack had to believe her, because Patty Magistrale was still in the picture, in spite of having permanently put away her viola. But as Jack said to himself many a time, Suzanne and Mac might as well be lovers. He was over at the house, or she was over at his place, at least once a week, and they were on the phone with each other at all hours of the day. At dinnertime Jack received a lot of the wisdom of Mac Delgado, and he assumed Patty must be getting an earful of the sayings of Suzanne Nelson. Now and then he thought about giving Patty a call to see whether she wanted to strike up a counter-relationship. After all, hadn't he always admired the intrepidness of Patty's style, her clunky old shoes and bad posture? But then he asked himself, did he really want to get tangled up, even in a friendship, with somebody else?

He went back over some of the afternoons he'd spent in bed with Elly and how charmed he was by her bold stories. He definitely didn't want Elly back, and he kept telling himself that she was a bitch. But then he'd remember a sweet gesture she'd made, or the plucky way she'd stood at the window that afternoon with the bedcovers clutched to her chest and her pretty backside right out there in plain sight. He didn't want to, but he missed the woman. And he felt that he'd hurt himself by getting close to her. When he thought about calling Patty, right along with that thought came a sensation that was like rubbing a deep bruise — except it was a bruise located inside, where he couldn't touch it.

It wasn't bad, though, being on his own. Or being with Suzanne when so much of her energy was directed toward Mac. Those two interested Jack. Did he know any other woman who had taken off her clothes *after* a young attractive man left her house? A little pain went with that part of his life, too, because his curiosity led him to ask Suzanne questions, and she was eager to talk, eager to tell him as much as she knew about what was happening with her and Mac. "We have a lot to talk about," she said. "Nothing to hide." Jack believed her. He almost wished he could catch her in a lie. It was more disturbing that the two of them were *not* having sex than it would have been if they were. But he discouraged himself from thinking too far in that direction.

What he really missed, though, was the music. Now and then he listened to his CDs, and he and Suzanne attended a few concerts. They even drove down to Middlebury to hear the Juilliard Quartet play at the college chapel, but Jack got so sleepy, they had to leave at intermission. Even though Mac and Caroline and Patty and Elly were local people, the Halvorson's had been a tonic — it woke him up. Jack shook his head when he remembered how they played. He knew he was lucky to have heard the Halvorson's at all. Its life was brief.

La Tour clears his throat. "You said we used to talk, Vivienne?"

"Yes, sir."

"What did we talk about?"

"You asked me questions, sir. I told you about my house and my room and what I liked to do and what I would eat if I went to Paris."

"Yes, I remember now. You said you liked a great deal of sugar in your coffee."

"Yes, sir."

"And a certain confection — almond, was it?"

"No, sir. It was hazelnut. I tasted it only once — in a café my parents took me to in Nancy when I was a little girl."

"Ah, yes, hazelnut. Vivienne?"

"Yes, sir?"

"I beat a peasant some years ago. I lost my temper. I shouldn't have done it."

"I'm sorry, sir."

"Also, when my wife was alive, I was sometimes unkind to her."

"I'm sorry for that, too, sir."

"And Vivienne?"

"Yes, sir?"

"Very soon I'm going to die. This week or next."

"Maybe not, sir. You've lived a long time."

"Yes, a long time. But you must understand, it isn't a kindness to wish me to live any longer. Even as greedy as I am, I know I don't need more of it. Wish me an easy death. Wish me not to be afraid."

"All right, sir."

"Please say it, Vivienne Lavalette."

Vivienne doesn't want to. It frightens her — it would be like reciting a witch's spell. She's about to say no, but the great tree stirs above her, as if it is taking a deep breath and shifting its branches. A breeze moves across her skin with skimming speckles of light.

"I wish you an easy death, sir," Vivienne whispers. She can't stop herself from looking at him as she speaks these words. "I wish you not to be afraid."

She imagines that La Tour says thank you, but she hears nothing. It's only that his lips move enough to mouth the two words. His eyelids come down, and she knows he's releasing her. Vivienne stands and puts on her clothes. As she dresses, the silence holds between them.

"Yes," the old painter says finally. "Yes, it was kind of you to come all this way to visit me. Will you put Caravaggio down for me?" he asks. Vivienne finishes buttoning her dress and steps forward to take the little dog from La Tour's lap. The coldness of La Tour's fingers brushing hers shocks her. The dog itself, however, is as hot as a brick heated by the fireplace. Its bulging eyes blink open for only a moment. When she sets it down on the grass, it is immediately asleep again.

"And now will you help me to the house, my dear?" La Tour stretches out his hand. "I can walk well enough, but since I lost my sight, I'm inclined to meander off in the wrong direction. The servants found me the other day wandering outside the gate. They made me promise to call them when I want to leave this chair. But of course I don't like to do that."

La Tour prattles on, leaning heavily on Vivienne's arm, while her mind reels against the disturbance of what he's just said. He can't see? He can't see! Something like rage flies up in her; he tricked her into taking off her clothes, and he couldn't even see her! But she can't sustain her anger, because she knows she's been lucky. Maybe she's the one who pulled off the trick. Didn't she take off her clothes and sit in front of La Tour for long minutes without the old fool knowing it?

The painter's blindness is a gift he's unwittingly granted her. This is the man who saw her naked and made her see the place on her shoulder. Now his vision has been taken away. The sight of her and her shoulder have been taken away, too. She helps him up the steps into the dark hallway at the back of his house — he's wheezing and putting so much weight on Vivienne's arm that she feels she's hefting a sack of old bones into the house.

"What — about — ?" he rasps.

"Yes, what?" Vivienne says sharply. She's impatient now, eager to be done with him. She walks him — pushes him — down the hallway and into the little parlor. La Tour waves his free hand, feeling for a chair. His breath rattles in his chest, and she can't wait to get her body away from his. When she finally does place him in position to collapse into a chair, it's all she can do not to push him there. Why she ever granted any power to such a helpless old creature she can't imagine.

La Tour's chest heaves, and he sits with both hands over it, his eyes closed and his mouth gaping. Vivienne steps back; she must get out before he dies in this very room.

"Picture —" he moans. He tries to lift a hand but can only flutter it against his chest.

"What?" she says. But then she remembers. "Oh, please don't worry about that, sir. I'll borrow my father's wagon to come by and fetch it tomorrow or the next day. Your servants can help me with it, sir. Please don't trouble yourself about it."

"I . . ."

"Sir?"

". . . sold — that — picture."

Vivienne can only stare at the despicable old man. His chest continues to heave, as if he's a beached sea creature. Amazingly, a hateful smile comes over his face.

"Money —"

Vivienne stands over La Tour for another moment. Then she walks back the way she came, through the dark hallway of the house into the day's last sunlight bathing the garden where they had sat so quietly. Here, too, she looks around a full minute before she moves to the side of the house and the path that will lead her to the gate. She feels as light as the air around her. Twilight isn't far away when she begins her dreamy stroll back through Lunéville toward the home of her father, Victor Lavalette, shoemaker of the village.

VI

O F THE MEN Elly had lived with, Jack was the best cook, by a long shot. There was a way he did swordfish on the grill — Elly told him he could make a fortune cooking that in a New York restaurant. But here was the thing. Jack's repertoire was limited. He could fix about a dozen meals. When Elly realized they were going through his cycle for the third time, she suggested a pasta dish she thought he'd do a great job with. He cocked his head and said, "Yes, I could probably do that, but what would be the point?"

Elly cocked her head in reply. "The point would be something different for us to eat."

Jack grinned and said that something different was what restaurants were for.

So they started going out every third or fourth night. It didn't hurt Jack's feelings that Elly didn't want to eat his cooking every night. And after a while the staffs at the restaurants got to know them as a couple, and Elly liked the idea that they had their own little place in Burlington; people recognized them; they were an item. She hadn't expected anything like that, but after about six weeks, she had a really giddy moment, walking out of Leunig's, when she admitted that she was happy. Not happy in some birthday-party kind of way. Happy like yesterday, right now, and probably tomorrow and the day after that. Happy like a huge pasture of happiness in every direction she looked.

The sensation was new. She thought of herself as having been around the block so many times, they were about to name it Elly Avenue. So it was more than a good feeling — it was the beginning of a major positive change. She figured that after about the age of twelve, you didn't get too many of those.

She didn't mention her pasture of happiness to Jack, in part because she didn't want him to take credit for it and because she didn't want him to feel responsible for keeping it in place. But mostly it was a private thing. *Life is good.* She believed it was fine to whisper that to yourself, but say it out loud, and you're doing a beer commercial. So she and Jack were walking down Church Street on a balmy evening, arm in arm, when he said — actually murmured in her ear — "One of these nights, she's going to be sitting at the next table."

And she said, "Who?" Because to tell the truth, at that moment Elly's thoughts did not include even one of Jack's ex's hangnails. But of course, to answer her question, Jack said the name aloud, *Suzanne;* murmured it as if it were a sweet nothing. Elly stopped on the sidewalk. Right then there were probably a hundred and twelve things Jack Nelson could have said to her, not one of which would have caused the destruction created by that little remark. With those two syllables, Jack shattered Elly's happiness into tiny pieces, right there on Church Street.

Yet she kept her cool. She wasn't about to admit that he'd just ruined her life. Still, his what-did-I-do? face told her he didn't have a clue about how to talk to his lover on a romantic evening stroll. She said, "Jack, your former wife can sit wherever she wants to. She can sit with her chin propped on my shoulder and watch me eat every bite of my dinner, but she's not going to spoil my appetite. That's how little she means to me. And you know what else, Jack?"

He shook his head.

"You're not going to be fit to throw out to the hogs until you start thinking about her exactly the way I do."

"'Not fit to throw out to the hogs,' Elly?"

That was a saying, she explained, her daddy used for somebody he considered worthless. "Usually it was a boy driving a truck or riding a motorcycle I wanted to go out with." And then, having had her say, she walked down the street. Jack stayed where he was, but Elly didn't mind; it meant that she'd got through to him. She kept walking.

"Elly," he called. "I hate to tell you this, but the man in your life right now is likely to remain unfit as hog food. I left Suzanne for you," he shouted out down Church Street, making a spectacle of them. She turned to face him. She could tell by his voice that his lips were trembling. "I did that," he shouted. "But that doesn't mean I have to purge her from my thoughts. I spent thirteen years of my life with her. I lived with that person. We weren't roommates — we *lived* together! What do you think that means to me?"

"Doodly-squat," she said, the words flying out of her mouth quick as bats out of a cave. She knew she'd gone too far.

Jack didn't move closer, but he was shaking his head at her. "You go on ahead, Elly," he said. "Take the car, and go on home or wherever you want. I've got to think about this for a while." And he turned in the direction they'd come from and started walking. She watched; he didn't look back.

That was the first fight she and Jack had had since they'd moved in together. Elly told herself she should have expected it. It irked her that in the infamous Church Street squabble between Jack and Elly, the real winner was li'l ol' Suzanne, probably sitting all by herself at home. Elly didn't drive back to the condo; that's what a wimpy wife would do and, she was certain, what Jack wanted her to do. Instead, she drove down to Waterworks and sat at the bar and carried out a little margarita research. She knew what Jack had in mind; he was no mystery to her. He was going to walk down to Waterfront Park and stand morosely by the lake, with his hands in his pockets. He'd do that for maybe twenty minutes. Then he'd set himself the project of walking all the way back to their place. It would take him a couple of hours, and Elly wanted him to get there before she did, so she'd have to pace herself, because even though she could drink a tub of margaritas, she didn't want to pick up a drunk-driving ticket. She was killing time at the bar, chatting with the bartender and this person and that, but was also reckoning with the revelation of the evening. No matter what she did with Jack or how good a time they had together, his ex was going to be right there with them. Silly her, for not having taken that into account. Or maybe she hadn't figured Jack to be such a victim of sentiment. "Definite oversight," she whispered to herself.

When she got back to the condo, Jack of course had been there for maybe half an hour, forty-five minutes — long enough to get himself good and upset. He'd thought he'd come limping in, exhausted from his long trek, and Elly would greet him with a thousand apologies and every variety of care and homey mothering oh-bubsies. What did he get? nobody home, air conditioning turned up high, and the new furniture he still wasn't used to. That was one cold place he'd walked into, Elly knew, which was fine with her. She also knew Jack had been worried about her and mad at her, and that the whole evening had made him pretty frazzled. And all that was fine with her, too.

"Jack," she said, first thing — she didn't give him a chance to start his story, because she didn't want to hear it. "Jack, you and I are going to put ourselves on a program. I can't ask you to purge your ex-wife from your thoughts. I know that. A person thinks what he thinks, no matter who says what. But you can *share* your thoughts. You can tell me so much about that woman that either we'll both have her on our minds — she'll be our mutual project — or we'll get sick of her, and she'll be gone."

So in the first weeks of the sharing program, Elly learned more than a few things. Jack's former wife couldn't start her day without taking a shower. After her shower, she got on the scale. If she weighed more than 130, she didn't eat dessert for the whole week. She took her coffee black — two mugs every morning — and she alternated between hazlenut and Colombian Supremos. She didn't like to talk in the morning. She didn't like sex in the morning, either, but she did like it in the afternoon, especially in the summer, when it was hot. She had a thing about bad breath, other people's and her own. She brushed her teeth after every meal. Before she went anywhere, she used Listerine. She flossed every night. She always washed her hands after she went to the bathroom. She hated that her deodorant stained the underarms of her blouses, but she wouldn't change it. She went through a phase of going to the movies by herself in the afternoon — she told Jack those were the only circumstances when she didn't mind crying. She didn't like the female superior position, but she did like . . .

Jack was willing to tell all. He couldn't get enough of talking to Elly about his ex. And evidently he knew enough about her to go on talking indefinitely. Elly might have been upset, except that she was impressed by how much he had to say. And in spite of herself, she was interested.

Because of the project, they were getting along fine. It was Jack's dream come true, talking to Elly about Suzanne. It put him in a great mood; he became very affectionate and more than a little horny. He'd call Elly from the office, his voice all husky, saying he couldn't wait to see her. What he really liked to do, first thing when he got home, was waltz Elly into the bedroom and under the covers and then begin talking. The talking and the foreplay started happening together. This was the part that finally got to Elly — because she let it go too far. Jack liked doing it with her while the two of them talked about Suzanne — how she fixed her hair, the way she painted her toenails before they went to the beach, her system for keeping her clothes in her dresser. Elly had done unusual things in a bedroom, but having this particular conversation during sex struck her as the most perverted act of all. First or second time, she had to admit she got into it. Jack was a wild man, and his excitement was contagious. It was only when Elly gave it some thought that she asked herself, *What am I participating in here?*

She assessed her sharing project and decided that it didn't start anything new in Jack. It simply revealed what was already there. And she began to catch on to her role: she was helping Jack move to the next phase of his relationship with Suzanne.

It was a Saturday afternoon when the light broke through to Elly. She and Jack were in the sack, in their post-coital mode, lying curled toward each other, lightly touching, as they fell asleep. Except that this time, Jack hadn't started any Suzanne conversation. As a matter of fact, neither had had much to say; they had concentrated on the sex — focused and businesslike — which was fine with Elly. Afterward, as they were lying there, quietly and peacefully, out of nowhere Jack whispered, "Do you know what she liked? She liked the sadness. She liked *after* lots better than she liked *during*. And the reason she liked it, she said, was that it made her blue. She said it was the purest thing; it made her understand . . ."

Until then, Elly'd thought their problem was nothing that couldn't be fixed with a good dose of frankness. She knew what was wrong with Jack's marriage: it was full of bullshit. He and his wife had been lying to each other for so long and about so many things that they were doomed to drift farther and farther apart. So she'd made Jack take a vow with her that they would hang on to the truth no matter what it cost. And she thought they were doing all right. They'd openly acknowledged that Suzanne was on Jack's mind; the sharing project put it right out there for them to deal with. They were talking honestly to each other — she knew she wasn't wrong about that. And their sex life couldn't have been better. What she hadn't reckoned with was that Jack would be moving closer to Suzanne all the time.

When he lived with his wife, he couldn't get close to her. Now that he lived with Elly, he was getting intimate with Suzanne. Right at that moment, he'd been as close to Elly as was physically possible, and what was he doing? He was loving Suzanne for the sadness she'd said she liked. If Suzanne had been the one lying there beside him, well, he'd have probably been irked that immediately after making love with him, she was a little depressed. But since Elly was the one beside him, he could give himself over completely to the appreciation of his former wife's quirky ways.

Elly heaved up the covers and started laughing. "Hey, Jack," she said, getting out of bed and heading for the shower, "you'll never guess what I just figured out." And she shut the door without saying anything more. It wasn't necessary.

VII

ONG AFTER he should have been dead, La Tour
sends a messenger to plead with Vivienne. "He says to
tell you, please, to come to his house. He begs you,"
announces the boy, acting with his face and his voice
to suggest the desperation of La Tour's request. Then the sly
boy smiles innocently as he claims that La Tour promised him
Vivienne would give him something for delivering these words
to her. The boy extends an unwashed hand and wiggles his
fingers.

"Go away, urchin," Vivienne orders. When the boy approached her, she was behind the shop, using her father's soft-
ening hammer to pound a new calf hide. Now she whams the
heavy thing down on the hide hard enough to shake the earth
beneath the boy's filthy feet.

He spits, missing the hide by very little. As she raises the
hammer again, he backs off, but before he rounds the corner of
the building, he stops and shouts, "The old man wants you to
raise your skirts for him once more before he dies, mademoiselle. You'd better hurry. He'll go to the grave with those coins
still stuck to his palms." Then he disappears. She hears him

laughing with his friends, who must have been waiting at the side of the shop.

Three years ago such an incident would have brought her to tears. Today Vivienne merely smiles and thinks of ways to get back at the messenger. But since the boy used only words to try to wound her, and since he owns nothing more than the clothes on his back, she won't waste more thoughts on him.

Vivienne's Maman and Papa are dead. In the middle of the summer last year, while her father took his afternoon nap on the bench beside the shop, his heart stopped. His pipe stayed in his hand, and he didn't make a sound. When Vivienne went to rouse him, as she usually did, she knew he was dead the instant she put her hand on his shoulder. Then, at the end of winter, her mother caught a fever and gradually weakened into stillness as spring came to Lunéville. It is August now. Not yet twenty years old, Vivienne feels like an old woman, as if she had caught her mother's age like the fever.

She has become the sole proprietor of LAVALETTE SHOES. Her Papa must have had an intimation of his early death, because he had carefully arranged the documents necessary for the shop to pass into Vivienne's hands. There's no debt on it. The old official who explained the details also informed her that an account of money is hers, too. Apparently, every week, from the time she was a baby, her father had dropped off a few coins at the man's office for his daughter's dowry or her inheritance. So even though she is not wealthy, she will be protected from poverty.

Vivienne knows that she could sell the shop; she could hire an assistant or an assistant *and* a manager; she could leave Lunéville if she wished to. And maybe she will. If she were to go to Paris — the thought teases her — maybe she'd regain her youth. But now she has no choice but to keep the shop and fill the orders taken by Papa from the villagers for shoes and boots. She's surprised to find she possesses the skills and the knowledge to be, as her Papa was, the shoemaker of Lunéville. Villagers tell her she must be the only woman in all of France who does this work. The shop is busier than it has ever been.

For many months Vivienne has not thought of La Tour — or, if she has, only fleetingly. The last time she saw the old painter, he was blind and feeble and appeared to be down to the last breaths fate had allotted him. Why wasn't he dead? She has lost her dear Maman and Papa; why is that treacherous old demon still alive? And sending for her? What a thing to hear — La Tour wanting to see her, begging to see her. *You've seen me, old man! You've seen me already!* she wants to shout at him.

Suzanne began to regard the house as her teacher. It was hers; she had it to herself. The way the sunlight slanted through the windows onto the green carpet was a lesson she could ponder for a whole morning. It was late summer, a day or two before she had to think about being in the classroom again. Jack was out of the picture, Mac had moved to California, her stint as department chair was over, and suddenly Suzanne couldn't figure out what to do with all her free time. "The name of this course is Solitude 101," she informed Sam one afternoon. The dog was following her as she moved restlessly from her spacious living room to her spacious dining room to her spacious kitchen. "My enrollment is strictly involuntary and, so far as I can tell, permanent." Sam wagged his tail, which made her wish she'd insisted on Jack taking him to live with him and Elly. "Sam," she said, "the last thing I need in my life right now is a dog wagging his tail. It's not an image that works for me." Still, as she lectured the tail-wagger, it occurred to her that the dog was absolutely in touch with his needs, whereas she was adrift within herself. "Don't have a clue as to what my needs are these days, puppy," she said.

What I need is exactly what I don't want, she told the empty living room. *I should give a party, fill this house with drinkers and chatterers, just to remind myself how hateful human company is.*

In a *Smithsonian* article on artists' retreats, she found a quotation she couldn't resist taping to the wall over her desk: *The cure for loneliness is solitude.* She wanted the comfort of that sentence in rooms other than her study, so she printed a copy for her refrigerator door. And the words became so prominent in her mind, she wondered whether she would say them during discussions with students and colleagues. She warned herself to be careful; otherwise they'd think she was hinting about her loneliness.

When she noticed that she was losing weight, Suzanne used the solitude quotation as a reminder to eat more, to open the refrigerator and have a snack. But she was rarely hungry. A yogurt with some fruit was usually all she could manage. Even thinking about eating had become a chore.

Sleeping was also an issue. She wanted to sleep all the time. If she lay down, she found it easy to drop off into a little half-nap. In a few minutes, however, she would snap awake and stay that way until the bed hurt her body no matter which way she lay. Although she liked Sam to sleep at the foot of her bed, because he slept so deeply and naturally, he often fell into dreams that made him twitch and whimper. Even when he slept on the floor beside her bed, he woke her with his licking and scratching — and sometimes with the tinkling of his dog tags. So at bedtime, she had to shut him in the breakfast nook downstairs, as Jack used to do. "I'm sorry, puppy," Suzanne said each night when she "put Sam to bed."

At a few minutes after midnight on the morning of September 16, three months after the divorce became final and perhaps a year since she'd spoken with Jack on the phone, he called. He didn't apologize. "I knew you'd be awake," he said. "How are you doing? I hear you're not getting out very much these days. I'm worried about you."

"I'm in bed, Jack. The lights are out."

"But you weren't asleep."

"I wasn't asleep; yes, you're right about that. I was maybe five or ten minutes away from being asleep. And now I'm probably two or three hours away from being asleep. So I imagine that concern for me is not the reason you called, Jack." Suzanne had her voice pitched as she wanted it at the moment — aloof and mildly irked. The fact was, she was delighted that Jack had called — and especially that he had called her at such an inappropriate time. Still, the last thing she wanted was for him to know how much his voice pleased her. She was glad she didn't have to see his face; that would have complicated things. A thought came to her that was so thrilling and delicious she had to speak it aloud. "Jack, Elly's out of town, isn't she? That's why you're ringing me up. Elly's gone, and you can't sleep. Isn't that it?"

The ticks of silence told Suzanne that he was deliberating over how to lie to her. With only the silvery streetlight filtering through her bedroom curtains to cut a pewter shadow across the foot of her bed, she savored the moment. She had caught Jack in a deviousness as she'd never caught him when they were married. She felt exuberant and reckless. "The night is long," she intoned dramatically into the phone. "Many a man at the break of dawn has prayed to know what possessed him to act in darkness as in the light of day he never would."

"What? What are you talking about, Suzanne?"

She laughed. "That's a quote, Jack. If you were better educated, you could snap back 'Alfred, Lord Tennyson' or 'Mark Twain' or —"

"Suzanne, this doesn't sound like you."

Heat springing to her face and neck jolted her up to a sitting position. "What would you know about how I sound? Oaf! Buffoon! Laughingstock of the city! If you had the slightest capacity for discerning human nuance, if you had even an elementary version of a perceptive apparatus, you wouldn't be the man who's being led by the *cock* all over town by Elly Jacobs!"

Suddenly she realized she was squeezing the phone with both hands and screaming at it. She slammed it into its cradle and sat in the dark, trembling, heaving to catch her breath. She wanted it to ring again.

It did.

On the fourth ring she picked it up but said nothing.

"I'm sorry," Jack said.

She still didn't speak.

Jack snuffled.

"Oh, hush," she said.

He was quiet, though she so clearly imagined him wiping his eyes and his nose and taking a deep breath that they might as well have been in the same room. "How's Sam?" he finally said.

"Are we really going to talk about the dog?"

"I don't know. I miss him. Do you mind telling me about him?"

So she did that. She told him a little Sam story, about how the thunderstorm last week so frightened the dog that he pushed his way through the breakfast nook's swinging door and came up to the bedroom to be near her. As she spoke, Suzanne felt herself relax. It soothed her to lie in the dark and talk to Jack about the dog. When she finished the story, she said, "I think that's it, Jack. I need to go to sleep now."

"All right," he said.

When she put down the phone, she fell quickly asleep, and only the next morning, after she'd been awake for a while, did she remember that neither of them had said good night. It seemed peculiar when she thought about it, but that's the way it happened. The rest of Suzanne's day resonated — rather pleasantly, she admitted — with her memory of the call. Evidently she was on Jack's mind — she was on his mind enough that when he got the chance, he couldn't resist picking up the phone and calling her. She was pretty certain he'd call again.

The problem was that now Jack was on her mind, after she'd thought she was at last reaching the point where she wouldn't think about him so obsessively. In their last couple of years of marriage, he had hardly crossed Suzanne's mind, but the day he walked out of their house, he began using up huge portions of her mental energy. Their late-night talk released some of her bitterness toward him, and she was amused to note that what she now remembered about him was on the positive side of her mental Jack-ledger.

After she sends away the messenger, Vivienne grumbles to herself as she works. When she closes the shop and goes to the kitchen to fix her supper, she continues to rage silently at La Tour for meddling in her life again. But when she sits down to her dish of sausage and potatoes, she breaks into sobs. It's as if she has to grieve for her parents again. Or was it that when she was grieving for them, she forgot to grieve for herself? Her childhood is also dead — and so beloved to her now, with the fragrance of her supper wafting up into her face. Her deep melancholy forces her to believe she must oblige La Tour. By the time she recovers from this renewed mourning, her supper is cold.

Early the next morning she hangs the CLOSED sign on the

shop door and sets out. This is a choice. She could take Papa's horse and wagon; they belong to her now. She could even hire a driver and put on her Sunday dress and present herself as a lady to La Tour. But she knows that if she is to visit him, she must make the journey as she did it at the age of fifteen, when her father told her that she was to go to him. When she arrives there, she wants to be sweating and fragrant, like the healthy village girl she once was.

Today there are no dogs on the grounds of the La Tour estate. Instead, the servants have apparently been waiting for her. Before — all those days she walked out here — these people were nearly invisible. Now a thin man in breeches and a white shirt opens the door for her, nodding as if he knows her, and a small girl fetches a cool wet cloth and a towel for her face. A boy brings her a cup of water. Then an old woman in a bonnet appears at the head of the stairs and beckons to her. Vivienne would rather have the dogs moiling around her feet than look into these obsequious faces. Heavily, she walks upstairs and follows the old woman to the door of the bedroom where La Tour is about to die. The old woman lets her in and closes the door behind her.

The room is dim and airless. Candles burn at the four corners of the bed. Vivienne approaches quietly — not the bedside but the foot of the bed. She wants to look at the old painter a while. He's blind; she can stare at him as long as she wants to. As she steps nearer, she sees that his eyes are closed. He's lying still, his bedcovers arranged neatly. In the huge bed, La Tour seems to have shrunk to the size of a schoolchild. Perhaps a barber was summoned to prepare him for his final hours, because there is no hair on his head or his face. The skin is as pink as a baby's. This withered creature bears so little resemblance to the La Tour of her past that she wonders for a moment whether it is the same man. But as she studies the mouth — sly even in his sleep — and the hatchet blade of a nose, Vivienne acknowledges that it could be no other than the artist for whom she posed.

"Sir?" she says. She didn't walk all the way here just to stand and watch an old man sleep.

His eyes snap open, the pupils so clouded that they're nearly pure white. Vivienne shivers and takes a step backward.

La Tour's mouth curls upward and then downward in that snarling smile she used to take as evidence of his vast acquaintance with the world. "Mademoiselle Lavalette," La Tour whispers, "I've been waiting for you."

Vivienne is quiet, hoping he will tell her whatever it is he must say. Finally she loses patience. "Yes, sir?" she says.

La Tour swallows. "Vivienne." He enunciates each syllable as if correctly pronouncing her name in her presence is what he has been yearning to do. Will he die now that he has said the name? Suddenly his eyes widen and the cords in his neck grow taut; his head rises slightly, and she could swear that the bleached-out eyes are focused on her. "I would like . . ." he begins. "I would like you, Vivienne, to tell me what your Maman fixed for your breakfast this morning."

The question opens her memory of the long-past days when the two of them spent those many hours talking as he slowly worked on his picture. She recalls thinking once that he was trying *not* to complete it. Hundreds of days began this way, with La Tour asking her a question and Vivienne spilling out her answer with pure happiness. His question also rips open a grief that she is still carrying within her, the piercing memory of her mother hovering around her in the morning, wiping her hands on her apron and trying to improve her daughter's mood, to give her any little thing to eat that would bring her pleasure. Vivienne stands at the foot of the bed, squeezing her eyes shut.

"This morning my Maman made . . ." She hears herself, but perhaps it isn't she who is speaking the words; perhaps it is the liar who lives inside her, the wolf-thing that makes the hair grow on her shoulder. Whatever it is, she cannot stop it. The words come out of her throat of their own accord. "This morning my Maman baked a loaf of bread, into which she had placed the berries I picked yesterday. And she added a little sugar, so that the bread — ah, you should have smelled the kitchen as it baked — the bread was like a berry cake. And, oh, sir, I must tell you that this morning Maman began to confide in me the secrets of cooking that she had learned from her grandmother — a small piece of butter, for instance, pushed into the top of the loaf before it is placed in the oven."

Vivienne's sentences form a picture of her Maman cooking, and the picture pleases her so much that she's happy to go on even after La Tour's eyes close and his mouth goes slack. "This morning when I had finished eating my berry bread, Maman took down from the shelf each of her spice jars and told me how she uses the spice and where it comes from. She had me smell each one and put a dot of it on my tongue. As she spoke to me, I knew I was to remember all these things; she would tell me only this once. I begged her to slow down, but she laughed happily and went on. I couldn't help myself, sir; I interrupted her. 'Maman, have you had a good life?' Tears came to her eyes, and she said, 'Of course I have!' She went on to speak of what a good man my Papa is, how he is the best of all possible husbands, better than any man she knew in all of Lunéville. Then she put her finger to her lips so that we could listen to Papa talking to himself, as he does when he is working alone in the shop, and she put her hand on my arm and whispered, 'But,

Vivienne, I would not have loved my life so much had you not come to Papa and me. I could not have loved my life without you in it.' Those were the words Maman spoke to me this morning, sir. Because you asked that question, I know you must sense how happy I am today."

Suzanne has a theory about desire and work. To herself she'll confess experiencing lust when she witnesses a man working with competence and grace. It doesn't happen often and never lasts long, but she's particularly vulnerable to waiters at good restaurants. Not the haughty ones, not the garrulous ones trying to chat you up, but the quiet, efficient ones moving among tables of customers like big cats ambling through the forest. Once every year or so, in New York or Boston, she'll find herself watching a waiter at work, wondering what he'd be like in bed. He's always thin, wearing a tie and a white shirt with the sleeves rolled up. He's never older than about twenty-eight, and he moves as though he'd played basketball for his high school. He works well with people, but in his private life, he's an incorrigible loner. Too smart for his job, he'll get out of the restaurant business in another year or two, but at the moment he accepts that he was born to do this work. She imagines that after this guy has slept with you, he might or might not call you up in a day or two. He definitely doesn't want you to take him for granted.

One day Mac Delgado was nobody to Suzanne; the next day he filled her mind so much, there was room for little else. It wasn't because she'd witnessed him waiting tables at Halvorson's restaurant. In fact, she'd seen Mac at work there several times — and though he was profoundly skinny and wore white shirts with the sleeves rolled up, he obviously had no passion for the work. Mac took over her thoughts only after, sitting beside her husband, she'd watched him rehearsing with the Halvorson's String Quartet on a Sunday afternoon in her house. Mac was the leader. His whole body demonstrated that he lived for what he was doing right then. It was Suzanne's first crush on a musician — on an artist of any kind — and she was amused by how girlish it made her feel. Maybe because she'd never experienced this in high school, the intensity of her feelings toward Mac embarrassed her. Nevertheless, they were delicious; she wouldn't give them up unless she had to.

That was a crazy afternoon, having the quartet in her living room. They'd needed a place to rehearse, and Jack had invited them to their house — his and Suzanne's. At the time Suzanne didn't have a clue about Jack and Elly. Her own world was out of control. She was head of the Art Department, which was in a state of crisis, and she was struggling to keep her professional life in order. She spent that whole Sunday morning in her office, writing reports for the dean, and then came home to a living room full of people tuning fiddles and a husband trying to please everybody and getting in everyone's way.

She sat on the sofa to relax and space out for a while, and that's where she was, beside Jack, when the quartet suddenly ceased tuning up, and a tense silence settled into the house. And that's when the waiter from Halvorson's started talking in his low voice about Beethoven. What was it about him? How he held his neck and shoulders? As she studied him, she wanted to slip her hand right in there, under the collar of his shirt. The young man lifted his instrument to his shoulder and did a slow head-bobbing count to get the players going.

They started on that dirge — a piece Beethoven must have written for his own funeral to make sure that everybody was sufficiently grief-stricken over his death. But never mind the gloomy sounds; Suzanne's attention was riveted on the first violinist. She could imagine exactly how he'd look without his shirt, and she didn't even know his name until after the rehearsal was over. While they were playing — and while Mac talked in that low voice between the movements — Suzanne sat absolutely still, at last understanding what those screaming teenage girls of the 1950s felt when Elvis Presley performed "All Shook Up." As she sat beside her husband on the sofa, she posed herself a question: *What would that young man do if I threw my underpants at him?*

Toward the end, as he was playing an especially emotional part, she noticed his eyes flick in her direction. It happened again before the conclusion of the piece, and both times he caught her staring at him.

After the rehearsal, after Elly concocted her ruse to get Jack to drive her home, after Carolyn Wadhams said she had to fix dinner for her mother, after Mac nearly pushed his girlfriend, Patty Magistrale, out the door, reminding her that she had to get to her martial arts class — after all that social activity, Suzanne and Mac stood in the foyer, facing each other. It was as if, without speaking, without knowing each other's name, the two of them had collaborated on getting the house to themselves. The door was shut against the outside world. It was quiet, deep stone quiet.

"Look, ah, Mrs. . . ." he began. That was when she was sure; in his voice she heard what her body must have been transmitting to him — highly focused carnal urgency.

"Suzanne," she murmured, meeting his eyes. Neither of them looked away; they hardly blinked.

"Suzanne, yeah, I, ah . . ." he started again. This time he reached over to touch the inside of her wrist with the tip of a finger that only moments ago she had watched performing astounding gymnastics on the neck of the violin.

"Me, too," she said, catching his finger, then snaring the hand that went with it. "And I think we don't have a lot of time."

Suzanne led him up the stairway, the two of them nearly running as they reached the top and she led him to the guest room. She could hardly catch her breath, but she was out of her clothes and he was out of his in about forty seconds. Right there, on top of the guest room bedspread, they did the deed. She climaxed more quickly than she imagined anybody but a fourteen-year-old boy could manage, and ten seconds later Mac tensed and shouted, the two of them accomplishing the whole kit and kaboodle — which is how she thought of it forever after, *the whole kit and kaboodle,* a phrase that struck her as comically precise — in five minutes at most. Then Mac was propping himself over her, panting, sweating, and trembling, and Suzanne had her arms stretched down with a hand grasping each of his buttocks, pulling him into her as tight as she could. When she'd stopped shuddering enough to be able to speak, she let her hands collapse out on either side of her and said, "Mistake, you think?"

He grinned. "No. I don't think so. Are you about to make a snow angel?"

At first she didn't get it, but when she did — the way she'd spread her arms — she liked it. "We should talk," she said.

"I'll help you clean the place up," he said.

"Only if we do it in the nude."

"No problem," he said.

She'd been teasing, but nude cleanup turned out to suit them both. They carried their clothes downstairs; he dropped his on the sofa, and she scattered hers around the living room. In a distracted way, they cleaned the kitchen but forgot to straighten up the rest of the house. All the while they were talking and walking around the house, they were as naked as animals of the forest. Mac was rail-thin, milk-white, long-muscled, lightly hairy, and gracefully at ease with his nakedness. Suzanne didn't have the slightest concern about the neighbors peeping in.

Their conversation has stayed with her, too. Suzanne told him about her miserable adolescence in Carroll County, Virginia, and the two sisters who hated her guts, about how she accidentally signed up for an art history class at Hollins College and thereby discovered what she was to do with her life, even though it made no sense to her family or anybody in her hometown. "Every time I get nostalgic about my hometown, I think about trying to explain to my dad why I'm ready to spend the rest of my life studying the paintings of Georges de La Tour. Do you know what he'd say? He wouldn't even dignify what I'd told him with words. He'd snort and look out the window, and as soon as he could manage it, he'd get himself in front of the TV. 'I've got to watch "Jeopardy."' That's my whole family right there: 'We've got to watch "Jeopardy."'"

Mac told her about his mother, about how he'd known he was in love with her from the time he was eight or nine. "There were two years there when I wanted more than anything in the whole world to have sex with my mother. That's probably not unusual," he said, "but I *knew* that that's what I wanted, whereas most kids don't really know what the deal is, or they're in denial or whatever. Me, I knew I was a little motherfucker — or I would've been, if I could've figured out how to score. I was so hot for her. My mom, though — she's always been a real looker. When it came to the male species, she'd seen everything there was to see. I figure she knew what was up with me but thought it was cute, my paying so much attention to her. My dad wasn't around that much, and when he was, he was all preoccupied with what was going on down at the office. Flirting was my mom's main recreation, anyway, so she used me to keep in practice. In this kind of absent-minded way, she led me through that whole Oedipal phase. Kept me interested, but made me keep my distance. Then when I was twelve, I went to violin camp and got interested in Becky Hampton. That did the trick. When I came home, I was over it with my mom. Funniest thing — she seemed wistful for the old days when I'd hung around her all the time — but you have no idea how relieved I was. For a while there I was worried I was going to grow up a real pervert."

Suzanne had never heard anybody speak about lusting for a parent. She was thrilled. "You could imagine doing it with your mom?" she heard herself ask. "You could actually see it in your mind?"

Mac nodded. He was leaning against the stove, as calm as if he had on his clothes. It warmed her face to look straight at him, and he didn't seem to mind at all.

"On the big screen right up here," he said, tapping his temple.

"How close did you ever get? I mean to really . . . to the real . . ."

Mac grinned. "Well, I probably didn't get anywhere near close. But one scorching summer afternoon, when we were sitting at the kitchen table, talking about one thing and another, and my mom had on her bikini, I was really noticing it and thinking about it — seeing it in my mind, you might say. So I was about to give it a try. I had the words all figured out. 'Hey Mom,' I was going to say, 'want to go upstairs and turn on the fan and take a nap?' Not a bad line for an eleven-year-old, huh?"

"What happened?"

"Just as I was about to say it, my mom stood up and said, 'I've got to get some clothes on. This is ridiculous.' I've always wondered what she thought was ridiculous."

"What do you think she'd have done if you'd said it?"

"Laughed in my face."

Suzanne got a flash of Mac as the eleven-year-old whose face turned red when his mother walked out of the kitchen and left him sitting there alone. "Want to go upstairs and take a nap?" she whispered.

Mac was still leaning against the stove, and she against the kitchen sink, both naked — and she had a clear image of them running back up the stairs to the guest room. But when she saw him cut his eyes over toward the clock on the microwave, she shouted, "Oh, my God, you've got to get out of here!" She never stopped regretting having done so, because that was the last chance she had of getting in the sack with Mac. Well, actually they went to bed lots of times after that, but only for conversation. Mac wouldn't do it again after that afternoon. He was apologetic, and said it had nothing to do with her attractiveness or sexiness. It was just that all their talk had made them too intimate. So it was taboo — "like wanting to do it with your sister," he said. And she figured that he meant "mother," even though she wasn't quite old enough to be his mother — unless the woman had got pregnant at about the age of nine. But there was that age difference, and what could she do? Either the man wanted her or he didn't.

For a long time, Suzanne felt nostalgic about that afternoon with Mac, and it wasn't bad. For one thing, when she found out about Jack and Elly, what she felt for Mac was like a medication. What she felt for Mac, combined with his loving to talk to her, got her through that difficult time. They spent hours together — at his place, at her place, walking down by the lake, having coffee on Church Street, wherever. They talked about his family and her family and their corny senior proms and why she never tried harder to draw or paint and what he might do with his music so that he wouldn't have to wait tables for a living. They talked about anybody they saw who interested them and about secret stuff like nose-picking and farting and meanness they'd done to other people and old secrets. They saved up little items to tell each other. They didn't try to keep their partners from knowing how much they liked each other's company. Mac said he hated talking to Patty, though he guessed he loved her. At least he didn't have scruples about having sex with her. So Patty, who had access to Mac's body on a nightly basis, hated Suzanne, because Suzanne was the one who got all of Mac's conversation. Mac told Suzanne that. And as far as Suzanne was concerned, Patty had the better deal. Suzanne would have been willing to trade, though she liked the conversation well enough, but she didn't tell that to Mac. Still, the whole thing pointed up how deprived she was in her relations with Jack.

Jack would talk all day and all night, but he'd developed a gift for not saying anything. Or not saying anything that mattered to her. She hesitated to let Mac know that was how it was with her and Jack. Anyway, she figured he probably knew, without her telling him directly. Whatever she had to tell Mac, he listened and asked questions. He took her that much further in her thoughts. Suzanne felt she hadn't begun to understand her life until Mac asked her about it. "So you grew up in Appalachia," he said once when they were walking by the lake — "mountains like those over there." He pointed toward the Adirondacks. "Those people are self-sufficient, aren't they? They don't like to ask anybody for help. They're suspicious, and they have a thing about fresh water. Is that how your dad is?"

"What?" she said. "Where do you get this stuff?" She recognized, in what he was saying, a bizarre truth about her family and the people she'd grown up with, but she'd never thought it before.

"I've been reading up on bluegrass," he explained. "Where mountain music comes from and all that. You must have listened to the Carter family all the time you were growing up down there."

She shook her head; she hadn't. And when he walked her back to his place and played his Carter Family CD for her, and she heard Mother Maybelle singing "Wildwood Flower," she felt a burst of homesickness.

"Mac," she said. She was in an urgent state, and they were alone in his apartment. He was standing in that loose way of his, with his shirt collar open two buttons down his chest, and Patty wouldn't be back for hours. "Please, Mac." She'd never begged him, but she could hardly stand feeling as she did and being this close to him and not . . . "Can't we?"

"God, I'm sorry, Suzanne." Mac shifted his body as if he were suddenly aware of how it was affecting her. "I honestly wish we could."

She didn't feel humiliated, because she could see he felt terrible, too, though she guessed it was a different kind of terrible from hers. They *could* have done it, and it wouldn't have hurt anything or anybody, but she kept that to herself; she didn't want Mac to feel sorry for her. And in the long run — after Mac had broken up with Patty and found a job playing in the Disney orchestra out in Los Angeles, and after she hadn't seen his face for such a long time that it stopped being dear to her because she couldn't remember it clearly — Suzanne finally admitted that maybe it was better that they hadn't. Done it. Anymore. After that one time.

La Tour has sunk far down into his sleep, and Vivienne sits in silence. His breathing is very slow. She imagines placing the pillow over his face, pressing down, and holding it there — the old painter probably would struggle, feebly, for only a moment — but of course she'd remember having done such a thing for the rest of her life. She tiptoes away from the bed, aiming to slip through the doorway so quietly that she won't wake him. But she takes no more than two steps when the old man rouses in a grand snorting and snuffling. In too loud a voice, he asks, "And what about your Papa, Vivienne? Where was the good shoe-maker of Lunéville while your mother was lecturing you this morning?"

For some reason, the idea of speaking of her Papa to La Tour pains Vivienne more than it did to tell him about her Maman. She has in mind that frozen instant of the late summer afternoon when she went out and set her hand on Papa's shoulder and jostled him just enough to make the pipe fall from his hand at the very instant she realized he was dead. She remembers the lemon light against the whitewashed side of the shop and the bright green spindles of the bench her father had painted only a month before. If she now speaks of Papa to La Tour, she fears that this moment — morbid but precious — will dissolve, and she will no longer be able to call it to mind. Yet she wants to respond, to give him what he asks for.

"Oh, sir, I am somewhat shy in talking about my Papa," she begins. "As you know, sir, he is an old man —" Vivienne turns sideways so that those sightless eyes will not be on her; then she quickly crosses herself and goes on. "Sir, I am embarrassed to tell you this — because even my Maman does not know. You must promise you will never tell a soul what I am about to tell you. If this became known in the village . . ."

"Of course, my dear, I promise." Shaping the words, La Tour's mouth takes on the old crooked smile. She remembers how his face held this configuration when she came here years ago and loosened her clothing for him. In those days his expression excited her — she understood how precarious his mood was; it could evaporate in an instant or quickly turn to contempt. But it was also possible, with the right movement of her body or teasing in her voice, for her to sustain the focus and intensity of La Tour's attention.

"Sir, there is a woman."

"Vivienne, there cannot be!"

"Oh, sir, I wish you were right." Vivienne blushes, with shame as well as with a thrill at the evil of what she is doing. If she were to walk into the village graveyard and dance on top of her Papa's grave, it would not be as terrible as her betraying him for La Tour's entertainment. Yet she knows — oh, what a thing to know! — that if he were alive, Papa might well be amused. Perhaps, even dead, he is amused.

"Vivienne, it is not possible. You told me your Papa never leaves his shop except to go to Mass on Sunday morning and to take his nap each afternoon on the bench outside."

"Some weeks ago this woman came into the shop, sir — to have her feet measured for boots. She insisted that Papa measure the distance from her ankle to her knee and that he take into account the slenderness of her ankle and the shape of her calf."

"Ah, there must have been a raising of the skirt."

"Indeed, there was, sir, a raising of her skirt and her petticoats as she sat in the fitting chair! And this woman instructed my poor Papa to grasp her shin with both hands and use his thumbs and forefingers to measure that pretty muscle of hers she wished to show off with her new boots. Until that moment, sir, I assure you that neither my Papa's hands nor his thoughts of womanly flesh had ever wandered from my Maman. Old as he is, my Papa is innocent as a young boy, sir."

"Tell me about the woman, Vivienne."

"Oh, I dare not, sir."

"Tell me."

"You don't know her, sir. She and her husband are new to Lunéville. And very wealthy."

"The d'Harnoncourts?"

"I cannot say, sir."

La Tour's face is animated, and, to Vivienne's astonishment, he has raised himself to a sitting position. He has opened his milky eyes, and he blinks as if he is taking in a sight that excites him. "My servants tell me the d'Harnoncourts are worldly people. And that they are a handsome couple. Where was your Maman when this measuring of Madame d'Harnoncourt's foot was taking place? And where were you, my dear Vivienne? Were you perhaps spying on your Papa?"

"Maman was at market, where she always is on Wednesday afternoon, sir. And I was not spying, sir. I was sitting quietly in the room where I do my sewing. As you may imagine, I was curious to see the person who had come to my Papa's shop and was saying such flattering things about herself. Of course I have no respect for her, but the woman is very stylish, sir. I was observing her clothes — her long white gloves and her grand bonnet — when she issued the request that my Papa carry out his measurements in this certain way."

"But you were staying out of sight yourself, weren't you, my dear child?"

"I was, sir. I confess that I was."

"And is that not spying?"

"Sir, should you decide to give up your career as a painter, perhaps you could be an inquisitor for the church."

La Tour starts to laugh. Then his throat catches, and he collapses in a fit of coughing, his face turning deep red.

"Shall I call the nurse, sir?" Vivienne sees the possibility of escaping when the old woman makes her way into the room.

La Tour flutters his hand. She knows what he means — she is to stay where she is. She can pretend she doesn't understand

and call in the old woman anyway. Or, it occurs to her, she should show him that she does understand and then directly disobey him. She is not another of his servants. She reminds herself that she's a woman of property, the owner of a shop in Lunéville. Should she choose to do so, she could walk out of this room and hire a carriage to drive her all the way to Paris.

Vivienne stays where she is and watches La Tour's coughing fit subside. The longer she stands by his bed, the worse she feels. Will she never be free of this despicable old creature?

He widens his white eyes at her and croaks.

"Sir?" Her voice is soft but firm. She despises herself more than she despises La Tour.

"More."

"More, sir?"

"More about your Papa — more about the woman." His mouth curls in that hateful way; he's so certain she'll tell him salacious details to make life flame up in him again. She knows precisely what he wants. If she gives careful attention to telling the part about Madame d'Harnoncourt's raising of her skirts and petticoats, she can have the old painter sitting up in bed again in no time.

"Suzanne."

"Jack."

This time he phoned at a decent hour — nine-fifteen — and though she hadn't been waiting for the call, Suzanne was ready to talk to him. What surprised her was her exhilaration.

"I have to ask you something."

She knew what he was about to ask. But how was she to answer him? She had no idea.

"Would you do it again? I know it's not possible, but I mean if you could?"

"What are you talking about, Jack?" Of course she knew, but

that wasn't the question she'd been struggling with for the past couple of days.

"Us. The whole thing."

She tried to hear in his voice what was truly on his mind, but as well as she knew him, she couldn't reach it. "Including the dog, Jack?"

He laughed, but only with an audible effort. "Sam, too," he said. "Definitely Sam."

Suzanne let some silence float by, hoping he would say more. He didn't. But sitting with the receiver to her ear, Suzanne knew, with certainty, that she still had this place in Jack Nelson's life — she was the one person on the planet who knew the ten thousand things about him. Whether there remained an ounce of love between them, she still held so much of his life in her head. By now, he should have made Elly into that person, but apparently he hadn't. She was about to scream at him when she realized he was crying. It wasn't that she heard it, but that was the only thing that could have kept him from talking.

"Jack?"

He didn't reply.

"Are you still there?"

"Probably not."

"You really want me to answer that question, though, don't you?"

"It doesn't matter. To tell you the truth, Suzanne, I expected you to hang up on me. That's what I think you should do."

"It's an option; I know that."

She half-expected him to hang up. But the seconds ticked away. Suzanne's pulse started to accelerate.

"I had a talk with your father I never told you about, Jack."

The silence on the other end grew deeper. She knew she had his attention.

"That visit to New York before we were married? That was about the only time I ever talked to either of your parents. I understood pretty quickly that your mother didn't want to talk, and I also figured out why she was such a scary person: she was scared to death. Of everybody, but mostly of you and your father. And of me, too, a little, though I wasn't much of a threat. Could be the only person she trusted enough to speak to frankly was that hairdresser of hers — Robert, I think his name was. Remember how she treated me to a haircut the second day we were there? That's when I got a look at your mother in Robert's chair, all done up with a bib around her neck and him playing with strands of her hair and pieces of different-colored foil and goop from two or three tubes. I couldn't hear what they were saying, but the two of them were like best friends in eighth grade, trading secrets, chattering with a purpose. She wanted me to see her in that chair so that I'd know, regardless of what I thought of her, that she had a life."

Jack grunted enough to show he was still on the line.

Suzanne continued. "I kept thinking your dad had something to tell me but wasn't getting it out. Sure enough, our last day, you remember you went to take your shower, and you left the three of us having coffee in the dining room. Your mother excused herself right away, but your dad stayed at the table, and I did, too. He didn't waste a minute. As soon as your mom left the room, he cleared his throat.

"'We realize you're to become Jack's wife,' he said. When I told him he was way ahead of me, he surprised me with his look. 'I'm sure I'm not even half a pace ahead of you, young lady. But that's neither here nor there. What's important is that you understand our relations with Jack. Our son has put us on notice that we are to keep our distance. What may seem to you rudeness or insensitivity or even indifference is, in fact, our honoring his wishes. Regardless of how it may appear, we care about Jack. We care deeply.'

"'Yes sir,' I said. 'I'm sure you do.'

"He gave me that buttoned-up smile of his and cleared his throat again. 'When Jack called to notify us of his decision to leave Dartmouth — to drop out in the middle of the semester — his mother and I drove up there, right away. Lorraine and I checked in at the Hanover Inn, and Jack came over from his fraternity house to have dinner with us at the inn so that we could discuss what he planned to do. His mother was holding herself back from begging him to stay in school — she'd promised me she wouldn't do that. We both understood that he was determined to drop out, but I took it upon myself to explain to Jack the importance of his leaving the college on good terms, of not burning his bridges, and so on. And Jack was listening. It was hardly a bright occasion, but we were still a family, and we were talking our way through a difficult situation that promised to be temporary.

"'When the waiter brought the check, Jack moved it over to his side of the table. I reached for it, of course, but Jack touched my thumb with his index finger. It was an odd thing to do, both reaching for the check and stopping my hand with that one finger. You see, until then, there had never been an occasion when I had not paid the restaurant bill. I certainly had no intention of provoking him. In fact, when he touched my hand, I dropped it on the table. Jack didn't move his finger; neither of us pushed against the other. There was the slight touch of his fingertip on my thumb. Someone passing the table might have thought we were expressing affection. Lorraine looked at our hands and then at Jack's face. That's when I raised my eyes, too. The look he gave me was scalding.

"'"Stop it," he said. '"I want you to stop."' He was sweating.

"'All right, son,' I said in a whisper. I wanted to tell him to let me know whenever he needed my help; to remember always how important he was to his mother and me. You can imagine most of the things that occurred to me. But I said nothing. I had thought I was maintaining my calm in the face of my son's challenge, but I recognized that the emotion welling up in me was beyond my control. What I saw in his face — perhaps what I felt from his fingertip still touching my thumb — shook me. I was acquainted with basic family psychology, and occasionally I'd experienced some tension in dealing with Jack. I don't think he was expressing hatred, but it most surely was rage — rage that must have been building in him throughout his boyhood. I was no more prepared for it than for a stone thrown through my living room window.'"

Suzanne paused — she could hear Jack breathing. "Your father and I sat there for a while. I thought he might sob, Jack, but what he did was more shocking, probably because I didn't expect it. I had my hands clasped on the table; it was as if the two of us were sitting there meditating. I was imagining how it must have been for you to grow up with that man as your father and what it was for him to have you as his son. That's when your father reached over and touched one of my hands with his index finger. It was as definite a touch as you could give somebody without its being a jab, but it was there and gone in an instant. I could scarcely believe he'd touched me. Then he stood up and said, 'You'll have to excuse me, please.' He walked around the table and left the dining room. He *strode* out of the room, in his pressed jacket and striped tie — you know how he is. But I knew what he'd meant me to understand. I'd taken him to be a man of little emotion, and he had shown me how wrong I was. His feelings for you, Jack, are powerful."

Finally she made herself stop talking, and the line was quiet a long while before Jack spoke.

"My dad just died, Suzanne."

"Oh, God, I'm sorry. I didn't know." But the minute she said it, she thought she *had* known. Maybe she knew Jack so well that when she picked up the phone and he spoke her name, the very texture of his voice informed her what was on his mind.

Again the line was silent; Suzanne held her breath, wondering whether Jack would say her story about his father was a lie. Would she admit it or deny it? As far as Jack was concerned, it probably made no difference.

"I'm going down tomorrow," he said. "There'll be a service at Saint Thomas's."

"How's your mother doing, Jack?"

"My mother is indestructible."

"So was your father."

"I guess you're right. I'll try to keep that in mind. You know, Suzanne, my memory of that night in Hanover is pretty hazy. I think they did drive up when I called to say I was dropping out. But I swear I don't remember that business about reaching for the check and what I said to my dad and all the rest."

Suzanne kept quiet. She couldn't risk saying anything to make him more suspicious than he already was. Jack's pause was long.

"But I can see it." His voice was as slow as if he were speaking his thoughts aloud. "Even if he was lying, I can see it just the way he told you." He laughed. "So the old man had a talk with you, huh? God, I never would have figured it. For me, he never had more than about three sentences at any one time, and at least two of them would have been his 'considered advice' on some topic I didn't want to talk about."

Jack's tone of voice conveyed to Suzanne that he was okay about attending his father's funeral. So even if she hadn't quite known what she was doing, she'd turned Jack in the right direction. But something else was happening, too, something she wasn't prepared for. She'd have to think about it. She was releasing Jack back into his own life. Did she want to? Did she want him not to need her anymore?

"Hey, Suzanne?"

"Yes, Jack?"

"He was a pisser, wasn't he? The old man?"

Now she laughed. A pisser was precisely what that old man was not. Still, she had to give herself credit — she had it in her to make Jack believe his father cared about something beyond the boundaries of his own skin. What was to keep her from unleashing the same amazing force into her own life?

"Goodbye, Jack."

She could tell that he wasn't quite ready to say it. But then he did. "Goodbye, Suzanne."

Vivienne breathes deeply. "My Papa . . ."

The room is quiet.

La Tour whispers, "Yes?"

"My Papa is dead."

Vivienne feels as if her head has been locked into the curve of a guillotine. The heavy blade has just begun to fall toward the nape of her neck. As quickly as she can utter it, she forces herself to say the other necessary sentence.

"My Maman is dead, too."

La Tour's bed — she holds tightly to the foot — retreats from her; dizzy as she is, she can't break away from the old painter's sightless stare. Now his bed seems to rush toward her, and he's fluttering his hands in signals she can't fathom.

"Sir?" she hears herself say.

He flaps his left hand toward the door.

"Sir?"

"Go!"

The word shocks Vivienne. Then it grimly amuses her that she's never imagined La Tour's commanding her to leave his presence. Perhaps she hasn't entirely lost her youth, because this is the vanity of the fifteen-year-old painter's model.

"My Papa —" Vivienne's voice is so shaky, she must begin again. "My Papa, who seldom had a harmful wish, died in the sunlight of an August afternoon, sir. The pipe that fell from his hand had been smoked halfway down — later, in my deepest mourning, I examined it — and because he had explained to me that the smoothest smoke of a pipe came from the middle of its packing, I am pleased to think that death came to my Papa in the few moments of the day that brought him greatest pleasure. Another puff or two from the pipe, and he would have let his eyelids ease down; he would have sunk into his nap as you or I would enjoy a warm bath. That is when death took him. And, sir, during my entire lifetime, my Papa loved to deny that he slept on the bench beside the shop, though everyone in the village knew he did. It was his little game with all of us, customers and family alike. 'No, no,' he would say to Maman, 'you are mistaking contemplation for sleep. In those minutes I sit on the bench, with my eyes closed, I am the great philosopher of my age. You see, I can think deeply for only a minute or two of each day before I must return to my job as the maker of boots and shoes.'"

Vivienne feels as if the painter is staring at her. Now he slowly shakes his head.

"It was not a bad thing, sir," she murmurs. She's surprised — she hasn't expressed the thought even to herself. "My Papa probably didn't know the difference, sir. He may have thought it was sleep coming over him, as it always did at that time of day. When I found him, there was no pain on his face, sir."

La Tour's face is distorted. With a mighty heave, he raises his head and rasps at her, "I don't want —"

Vivienne obeys her impulse to step to the side of the bed and grasp La Tour's hand. Because it is so cold and heavy, she marvels at it — and remembers that the last time they touched was when he asked her to show him her hands on her first day in his studio. She can feel him wanting to pull away from her, but then the tension leaves his arm and wrist. She sits on the side of the bed and holds the old painter's hand between hers. She rubs his hand as if to warm it, though the chill is as permanent as a stone's.

"My Maman was different, sir," she says softly. "Maman knew her death was approaching, and she wanted to talk to me about it. I thought it my duty to argue with her. 'No, no,' I would say, just as my Papa loved to say the same word twice to her — as if contradicting her was his way of saying how much he cared for her. "No, no, Maman,' I would say, 'you have years and years of life ahead. And who would look after me if you were to leave now?' Though I meant to tease her, I know now that was not nice of me to say, because my Maman's greatest worry was that I would not look after myself. She would try to instruct me about the kitchen and the garden and the way to store potatoes in the coolest part of the cellar and how to talk to the butcher and what to do with milk that's old, and how much salt to rub into a ham, and where to look for mushrooms at a certain time of the year. Until the last morning of her life, Maman tried to give me the thousands of scraps of knowledge she had stored inside that head of hers — and I'm afraid I haven't remembered a single one, sir."

La Tour has calmed, but his gray-white eyes are still directed toward her face. She thinks he's trying to whisper. "Sir?" She bends forward, putting her ear close to his mouth.

Vivienne is aware of something, though it takes her a moment to define the sensation. With the fingertips of his other hand, La Tour has brushed her hair. Because it is the briefest and lightest of touches, she doesn't pull away. She can make out some of his words.

"Don't — want — you — to — see —"

It comes to her, then, what is troubling him. She straightens enough to look at his face. "Do you want me to call in the nurse?"

Slowly he moves his head to one side, then back.

"Do you want me to leave the room?"

Again, he makes that movement with his head. She imagines he's trying to smile, though his face holds such sadness, she knows she's been crying for a while, perhaps since she started telling the truth about her father.

Vivienne continues to gaze at his face. When he lifts his eyebrows, she bends forward again.

"Turn — your — back!"

Now she understands him. She stays where she is, sitting beside him, with his hand, but she turns her face away.

It takes a long time. But when it happens, she can feel it, from his hand in hers. She recognizes the exact instant. For a while longer she holds the painter's hand without looking at him. When Vivienne does turn her face around, she's shocked at how the life has disappeared from his old face, along with what little color there was. The eyelids are half-open. She releases La Tour's hand and, with her thumb and first two fingers, holds the eyes shut long enough that they will stay closed forever.

3/02

McN

FIC
HUDDLE

3/02

Huddle, David,
1942-

La Tour dreams of the
wolf girl.

DATE			

BAKER & TAYLOR